# Missing Emma

## a Jenny Tallchief Novel

### E. H. McEachern

authorHOUSE®

*AuthorHouse™*
*1663 Liberty Drive*
*Bloomington, IN 47403*
*www.authorhouse.com*
*Phone: 1-800-839-8640*

*Published by AuthorHouse 8/24/2012*

*ISBN: 978-1-4772-6028-9 (sc)*
*ISBN: 978-1-4772-6027-2 (e)*

# Acknowledgements –

*Thanks to the following for their patience
and professional assistance:*

**Michelle Cole, DVM** – *Veterinarian technical advice*
**Susie Cole** – *Story continuity and editing*
**Stewart Beasley, Ph.D.** – *Psychological profiles*
**Joe Scavetti** – *Research Assistant*

# Dedication –

*To my sister- and the special love that binds us.*

# Chapter 1

Jenny gave the door to the kennel a boot with her backside, effectively muting the cacophony of yips, yowls and barks from the multitude of smaller animals caged inside. Jenny suppressed a sneeze. Springtime in Oklahoma was a season of sudden storms, raging streams and enough allergens to choke a horse. "In fact," Jenny thought, "I'd bet at least half of our patients suffer from nothing more than allergies."

As she leaned against the door for a moment, she pushed at a hair that had escaped from her long dark pony-tail and glanced at her long-time friend and companion, Jesse.

Jesse, half German shepherd and half collie, returned her stare with big, soulful brown eyes that seemed to say, "You work too hard. Slow down."

"I know, I know – just one more and we'll go home."

Jenny knew her last patient of the day would not

be an easy one and wondered if mentally she had been postponing dealing with the irritating Siamese owed by Naomi Miller. Not only was "Sissy" an uncooperative and obnoxious animal, she was also a frequent patient.

'I guess that's not all that surprising," thought Jenny to herself. Miss Miller herself was a hypochondriac, a trait she apparently had passed on to her cat. Worst of all, the mere sight of Sissy sent Jesse into a rage, behavior totally unlike her usual gentle, go-with-the-flow attitude.

\*\*\*\*\*\*\*\*\*\*

Jennifer Lynn Cochran-Tallchief, D.V.M., was in her second year as a full-fledged veterinarian in the small town of Tecumseh, Oklahoma. She had been married to the youngest Pottawatomie County Undersheriff since her final year of vet med school at Oklahoma State University.

Six months ago 'Doc' Martin had taken Jenny on as his partner, because he was at a point in life where he wanted to spend more time fishing than tending sick animals. In Doc's estimation, Jenny had proven herself to be an outstanding veterinarian. She was young and eager – willing to work extra hours – which worked out perfectly for Doc as he was more than willing to fish extra hours. The two doctors had bonded in that special way only those who have a deep love of animals can.

\*\*\*\*\*\*\*\*\*\*

Although many in the community thought Jenny was full-blooded Native American, she was in fact of Scots-Irish and French descent - a heritage that could be seen in her sparkling blue-gray eyes and the long, dark hair that usually hung straight down her back. Her high cheekbones spoke to her ancestors from Gaul.

It was her husband, Caleb, who was half Cherokee—even though he looked like someone out of a WASP ad. When townsfolk would comment on his beautiful Cherokee wife, Caleb would laugh and say, "There's just no figuring genes."

Few, if any, caught the irony.

Doc Martin's place was a small clinic – just outside the city proper about a mile and half south on Kickapoo and half a mile east on Kimber Lane. The road running alongside the Clinic was marked as gravel on every map of the area, but generally it was just dirt or mud, because the county crews seldom made it out this far to put down fresh rock. The remote location put the clinic a little closer to the farms Jenny and Doc visited when one of the big animals needed their help. It also kept neighbors' complaints down when the domestic animals staying at the clinic got a little boisterous in their conversations.

But being so far out of the mainstream was lonely and Jesse was often Jenny's only companion - especially when Caleb was unable to stop by or Doc's fishing hole beckoned.

Tonight Caleb would probably be even later because of the five county alert for two escaped prisoners from McAlester. He'd been called out in the middle of the night – or rather in the predawn hours of this morning. The escapees had been sighted near the town of Allen, so most of the Pottawatomie deputies had been sent to the southeast corner of the county. The deputies were also on the lookout for any suspicious drug activity as there'd been a marked increase in the amount of meth traffic in PottCo. Sheriff Holcomb was trying to get a handle on it before it got out of hand.

So, Caleb may not even make it home tonight at all. Although he promised to call later, Jenny was sure it would be a long while before she heard from him. Perhaps that was one reason she didn't mind working late tonight at the clinic – at least she wasn't home worrying about her husband.

Dusk cut deep shadows across the reception room as Jenny bid their receptionist, office-manager and general do-it-all person, Annie Hawthorn, good night. Annie hurriedly collected her purse and scurried out.

Annie always left right on the minute of six. She could not wait to get home, although Jenny could never figure out why. Annie had a good-for-nothing alcoholic husband whom she loved absolutely and supported without complaint. And her fully-grown and chronically unemployed son also lived at home and mooched off his mother. Annie was fiercely protective of both – she had a bucket full of excuses as to why neither man could provide any income. Anyone even vaguely implying her husband or son were no accounts had better be prepared to endure Annie's wrath.

"Families are certainly odd creatures," Jenny thought.

The slam of the screen door, quickly followed by the loud wail of an ailing catalytic converter, signaled Annie's departure for the evening. The noise faded as the pickup exited the parking lot and headed west.

A hush descended. Stillness pervaded the clinic and even time seemed to slow. Tree frogs sang in the deepening dusk. "When it gets quiet in the country," Jenny said to her companion, "it really gets quiet."

In a moment Jenny snapped back to the job at hand. "Okay, Jesse. You know the drill. Come with me."

Jenny led the subdued animal to Doc's office. The layout of the clinic was simple. The reception area was up front. There were two small treatment rooms on the right side of the hallway and the surgery and Doc's office on the left. A general all purpose area containing storage, work desk and computer station was tucked into a corner of the kennel in the back.

Entering Doc's office, Jenny opened the door to the large crate by the radiator behind Doc's desk. The radiator hadn't worked in years. In fact, the clinic had central heat and air, but for some reason, the old fixtures had never been removed.

The same contradiction could be found throughout Doc's personal space, modern next to old, state-of-the-art adjacent to antique, cutting-edge propped up against useless.

"There's probably some deep psychological meaning to Doc's office," thought Jenny to herself, "but I really don't want to know what it is."

Jesse hung her head and tried to look pitiful.

"Well, I wouldn't have to do this if you could control yourself around Sissy," Jenny commented as the shepherd reluctantly and slowly entered her "cage."

Jenny didn't feel at all sorry for Jesse as she closed and latched the crate. She turned away without a glance at the dog's big brown sorrowful eyes and reentered the kennel to the accompaniment of the animal chorus.

As Jenny returned to the front of the clinic with Sissy in arm, she could hear Jesse's strident barking. "I guess she's getting warmed up," she thought.

But the barking was not a protest – it was a warning. Framed in the doorway between the reception area and the hallway were two unshaven, earth encrusted, menacing figures. They were dressed in prison orange and Jenny knew instantly these were the two escapees. How they had traveled across the several counties separating the prison from the clinic was anyone's guess, but here they were. And here she was - all alone.

Hello, there, pretty lady," said the taller of the two. Jenny could see he was about Caleb's height, 6' 1" and broad-shouldered. He could even be called handsome, but something about his lifeless eyes made Jenny shiver. The other, a small weasel-type man, sheltered in the shadow of his partner. He, too, emitted an aura of evil.

"I'm sorry, the clinic is closed." Jenny tried to maintain her composure – she didn't want them to know just how terrified she really was. In Doc's office, Jesse threw herself at the door to the crate, growling low in her throat between outbursts of ear-splitting barking.

Jenny dropped Sissy and bolted for the phone on Doc's desk. But before she could reach it, the big man intercepted her, shoving her away and pushing the phone well out of reach.

"You better shut that dog up – or I will" shouted the large man, as he flashed what appeared to be a home-made knife of some kind.

"Hush, please Jesse, *hush*," Jenny spoke to the dog in soft, pleading tones. Jesse sat uneasily, swiveling her head back and forth from one intruder to the other and back to Jenny.

As the noise from Jesse subsided, the larger man approached Jenny, grabbing her by the hair and pushing the knife against her throat.

"Well, little girl, this place isn't closed to us….we got us some needs and maybe you can help us out with that…what do you say? Money … you got any guns? Of course you do, every place around here has guns, don't it, Earl?"

"Shut up, don't be saying my name, Harlan," came the whine from the doorway.

"Oh Earl, this little gal ain't gonna talk, are you, honey? Of course not. Earl, you look around and see what you can find. I think me and this lady are going to have some fun."

The one called Harlan pushed the crude knife closer into the soft skin under Jenny's chin, and a trickle of blood oozed its way down the front of her white coat. His eyes took on a far-away look as he noted, "And I need me some fun - it's been a really long time."

Earl was more than happy to get out of there. He didn't even want to think about what Harlan was going to do to this poor woman. Time and time again, Earl had heard about Harlan's many exploits with the 'ladies.' It was one of those exploits that landed Harlan his life-sentence without parole when he was convicted of a particularly brutal rape and murder of a 15 year-old girl. And, according to Harlan, there had been many more "ladies" the cops never had found out about.

Lifting Jenny off the ground, Harlan spotted Doc's old decrepit couch. He half-carried, half-dragged her over to the corner and roughly tossed Jenny on to the worn-out leather. Then, with one fluid motion, he yanked the bottom half of her scrubs down to her ankles and climbed on top of her, settling himself between her knees.

Harlan grasped her throat with one of his large hands, and used the knife to cut away her underwear. As he pulled his pants down, his eyes became more distant, fixed on something faraway. A cruel smile teased the corners of his mouth. Jenny looked into those eyes, and, in that moment, she knew he would not leave her alive.

As Harlan roughly pushed into her, Jenny screamed. She didn't mean to give him the satisfaction, but she couldn't help it. Pain and fear washed over her in a great wave. Harlan burst out laughing as if there were some great joke only he knew. He punched Jenny hard in the face once and then again. He grabbed her hair and knocked her head against the wooden arm of the couch. Jenny struggled to stay conscious.

Jesse went crazy, growling, barking, snapping, and repeatedly ramming herself against the crate's latch. The crate rocked on its base with her fury.

Finally, the big man screamed, "Earl, get in here. Now!"

The last thing Earl wanted to do was to go into that room. But he dared not cross Harlan. Harlan may have been a lousy friend, but he for-sure was a God-awful enemy.

Lingering just outside the door to the office, but not looking directly into the room, Earl said, "What, man? I'm looking for guns and shit."

Harlan was using the knife to run a slit up the center of Jenny's scrub top and bra, nicking some of her skin beneath, all the while pumping into her. "I want you.....I want you to take that damn dog out of here and kill it!"

Jenny's bra fell apart, leaving her left breast partially

exposed. A shudder of excitement coursed through the large man. He shoved aside the remains of her top and cut a small circle around her nipple.

Earl let out a huge sigh and began to slowly and unenthusiastically edge his way over to the radiator, sidestepping with his back as close to the wall as possible, eyes averted from the horror taking place on the couch. As Earl reached close to Jesse, he carefully eased the big crate's latch up from its housing. "Oh shit!" he thought, "big mistake."

In the instant Jesse sensed the bolt come free from its base, she hurled forward, knocking the little man hard into Doc's desk.

In two running leaps, Jesse reached the couch and sunk her teeth into the bare buttocks of the man hurting her Jenny. Harlan screamed, came to his knees, twisted, and tried to stab the large dog. Sighting a better target, Jesse released her grip and bit Harlan's unprotected genitals.

Alert that this might be her only chance, Jenny shoved herself free from under the big man. She skittered across the floor on her hands and knees to Doc's desk.

Although Doc dearly loved all animals, he didn't have the same high regard for the human race. He kept a fully loaded .45 automatic hidden under some old papers in his bottom desk drawer– just in case. And, in this moment, Jenny blessed his attitude. She found the gun, released the safety and cocked it.

At the sound of the gun, Harlan swiveled and stopped his attack on the dog.

"Jesse, come." Instantly, Jesse was at Jenny's side.

"Now look, lady….." Harlan started to raise his hands. With no hesitation, Jenny emptied the entire clip into Harlan, hitting his head and chest, over and over, just as Caleb had taught her.

Transfixed from the moment Jesse had broken free until the sound of the last shot stilled, Earl took one last look at his friend, slumped on the couch, bleeding from his genitals, and sprinkled with bullet holes. He scrambled to his feet and almost flew into the hallway as fast as his churning arms and legs would carry him.

Jenny heard the front door slam open, followed by the clang of the screen door. Jesse started after the escaping man, but Jenny put her arm around the dog's back and held her close.

Jenny was stunned. Blood oozed from the back of her head, as she slipped in and out of consciousness. Jesse, also bleeding profusely from knife wounds, collapsed at Jenny's side.     Time passed.

**********

After what seemed to be an eternity, Jenny regained partial consciousness for one small, but lucid, moment. She knew she had to get help and get help fast. She grasped the phone cord at the wall and pulled it toward her until the phone crashed to the floor beside her. Doc may have been an old curmudgeon about some things, but thank God he loved his gadgets– including speed dial.

Jenny hit #1 and the phone immediately started to ring at Doc's home. After a ring or two Doc's grumpy voice came on the line, "Jenny, what the hell are you still doing at the clinic…..? It's after eight…"

Jenny tried to make herself heard, but her voice wouldn't cooperate…Doc could hear Jesse's whimpering and finally Jenny's whisper, "Doc, help…" and then nothing.

Doc grabbed his coat and cell phone on his way out the door, dialing 911, the sheriff's office and anyone else he could think of as he ran to his silver El Camino and screamed out of his driveway heading east.

At the clinic Jesse rested her head on Jenny's still body, watching over her, as their blood mingled and pooled around them.

# Chapter 2

As Undersheriff Tallchief approached his patrol car, he could hear the radio squawking, "Caleb, come in – Caleb, where are you?" Caleb picked up the mike, "Hey, Mary Ellen, what's wrong? I was out looking for those two escapees at the ravine by Clyde Johnson's place and...."

"Jesus, Caleb, get over to the clinic right away. Jenny's been hurt." Mary Ellen Moore never swore –the Sheriff's prim, very old-school Southern Baptist dispatcher was always proper and professional.

Caleb's heart constricted in his chest. He couldn't catch his breath. "What...what happened, Mary Ellen?"

"Just you get over there – and hurry!"

Caleb was already in motion. Flipping on the overheads and the sirens, he spun around in the dust of the roadside, skidding and spinning until he gained control on the blacktop of Route 39.

"Shit, I'm all the way on the other side of the damn county." For the first time in many years, Caleb felt panic. "What in the hell was he doing all the way over here when Jenny needed him? Please God, let Jenny be alright...." Caleb prayed silently over and over again.

The trip across the county was a blur. The few cars Caleb encountered leaped to the side of the road. Perhaps it was fear at the way this crazy lawman recklessly sped past. Perhaps the more astute recognized his desperation.

Caleb screeched to a stop in the clinic's parking lot, blanketing the whole area in a cloud of white dust. An ambulance was already on the scene; its flashing emergency lights illuminated the landscape in a surreal flickering lightshow. Doc Martin's dirty silver pick-up, engine still running, was parked askew in front of the clinic with the driver's side door wide open. Sheriff Holcomb was there circled by five or six men from Tecumseh.

The Sheriff broke away from the group and was headed toward Caleb, but Caleb ignored him and charged headlong into the clinic and down the hallway. There by Doc's desk and surrounded by paramedics, was Jenny, unconscious and covered with a bloody sheet. A young blue-shirted man was busy hooking up an IV and a second was relaying her vital signs to the hospital.

Holcomb followed on his undersheriff's heels. "Jesus, Caleb, I'm sorry. We're not sure what happened, but it looks like the two prison escapees found Jenny here alone. Looks like she killed one of 'em – Harlan Ray Lucas."

For the first time Caleb noticed the dead man sprawled across the old couch. He didn't look very tough now, in fact, he looked ridiculous with his pants down and a huge holes blown through his head and chest. Nobody had bothered to cover him yet.

"No sign of the other one, but we're sending out search teams now to round him up. He won't get away." Caleb looked at his mentor and friend, the unspoken question in his eyes.

"Looks like Lucas beat her up pretty badly and … he raped her, Caleb. God, I feel so damn bad about this - we'll catch that other piece of shit – I promise you that." Holcomb was fighting to hold back the tears.

Caleb knelt beside Jenny's still body and took up her hand. He whispered to one of the paramedics, "Will she live?" Caleb could barely get the words out.

"I don't know. She's lost a lot of blood. Sir, I'm really sorry, but I need some space here."

Holcomb took Caleb by the shoulder. "Let's stand over here and let the professionals do their work, OK?" Caleb reluctantly got to his feet.

Holcomb continued, "Looks like her dog got in the act, too. The shepherd was pretty badly cut up. Doc Martin stayed with Jenny 'til the paramedics got here. He's trying to patch up the dog right now."

Doc soon emerged from the adjoining surgery room and spoke quietly with the paramedics. After a brief exchange, Doc approached Caleb and Holcomb. "Looks like Jenny's vital signs are strong. She's lost a lot of blood, but she's in good shape and she's young. I know she's going to make it just fine."

"How's Jesse? Jenny really loves that dog." Caleb asked.

"I've sedated her and stopped the bleeding. I just need to take care of the more superficial wounds now. If everything goes okay, Jesse should heal just fine. Most of the cuts looked worse than they were."

Doc turned on his heel and took a few steps. He stopped at the surgery room door and looked back at Caleb, "I can't tell you how sorry I am. I should never have left her here alone – not with those crazies on the loose…"

Caleb walked over to the elderly doctor and put his hand on his shoulder, "It wasn't your fault. I think the man whose fault it is has paid the price – and the other one soon will."

# Chapter 3

Jenny's recovery was long and painful. The ravages her assailant inflicted had required two separate surgeries. The doctors couldn't promise Jenny would ever be able to have kids, and she and Caleb had both wanted a big family. Caleb had spent part of every day of the first few weeks with her in the hospital, holding her hand as she relived the horrors of the attack in nightmarish dreams over and over again.

Jenny lost her beautiful long hair. The surgery to repair the damage to the back of her skull required she have her head shaved.

Jenny's younger sister had made so many trips down from the university that she finally had to drop out of the semester. After checking out of the dorms, Emma stayed at the Tallchief home, watching over her sister when Caleb went to work.

The two sisters, close before, became inseparable. Their parents had died several years earlier – first their dad from cancer and then, as so often is the case with couples married for many years, their mother six months later. At age 20 Jenny took on the responsibility of raising her 14 year-old sister. She became mom, big sister, best friend and confidant. Now almost seven years later, their relationship was even stronger.

Caleb loved Emma almost as much as Jenny did. He had no sisters – only a six-pack of big burly brothers. From the start, Emma had become his kid-sister, too.

********

After Jenny's release from the hospital, their lives – at least on the surface - returned to normal. But the relationship between Jenny and Caleb was far from what it had been. Jenny had become increasingly withdrawn and skittish. Caleb, partly to make up for the time he had taken off for the past month, but more to avoid the hurt his presence seemed to cause Jenny, began to work as much as he could.

Keeping busy was no problem. On the day Caleb returned to work full-time, he and Sheriff Holcomb finalized plans for the upcoming meth drug bust that would be going down in two days time. After several months of undercover work, more than 100 law enforcement officers and agents from across the state were going to meet in Shawnee and from there spread out to raid meth redistribution centers throughout the county. The authorities would include the Shawnee police, the Pottawatomie County sheriff's deputies, local drug enforcement officers from the Oklahoma Bureau of Narcotics, Tecumseh police, Lincoln County sheriff's deputies, the Citizen Potawatomi Nation tribal police, and several U.S. Marshals. Two National Guard helicopters and their pilots were on loan to assist with reconnaissance.

Undercover agents had been conducting around-the-clock surveillance for the past two weeks. They confirmed extremely large quantities of Mexican methamphetamine were being brought into the area, taken to remote locations and repackaged for distribution throughout central Oklahoma. The plan was to hit the repackaging stations simultaneously so there would be no time for the drug network to spread the word about the raids.

Holcomb wanted Caleb to be the liaison with the unit hitting the Wood Creek area – as there were reportedly two large operations just outside the city limits. Dan Morgan, another PottCo deputy, had also been assigned to the Wood Creek unit. He would be part of the team that would strike the trailer west of Highway 102; Caleb's group was in charge of the location on the east side. Sheriff Holcomb would remain in Shawnee, at the command post.

At 4:00 am on Friday, all was in readiness. Each unit was scheduled to hit its target at 4:30 on the dot. Each officer waited anxiously – not knowing how many people would be inside – nor how many guns they would have at the ready. Although most of the men and women waited in silence, an occasional whisper or muted chuckle here and there relieved some of the tension.

At exactly 4:30, Caleb's team leader pounded on the trailer's door, announced he had a warrant, and demanded entry. A few seconds later a small bedraggled man opened the door. When he saw the number of police firearms aimed at him, he slowly raised his hands. He was alone in the trailer – alone with three pounds of the powerful narcotic.

The raid on the other Wanette location had not gone so well. Two of the five suspects in the dilapidated old house decided to run rather than surrender. They jumped from the second story window, firing wild shots in the general direction of the law enforcement personnel surrounding the structure. Deputy Dan Morgan was hit in the neck – just above his vest – and fell to the ground seriously wounded. One of the two suspects was shot in the hail of return fire; but both men were able to reach an old Nissan two-door and speed off toward the highway. OBN and Lincoln County deputies gave chase, radioing one of the helicopters for assistance. The helicopter picked up the Nissan's trail almost as soon at it careened onto Highway 102. The pursuing agents and deputies forced the vehicle off the road and subdued the fleeing men within 30 minutes of the action at the house. The suspect who had been wounded at the house was dead when the deputies pulled him from the passenger seat – bled out from the wounds inflicted at the meth house.

In all, the bust garnered 40 arrests, recovered fifteen pounds of meth and more than $250,000 in cash. The only injuries and casualties had been those resulting from the west Wood Creek raid. Deputy Dan Morgan was air-lifted by the Oklahoma Guard helicopter to St. Anthony's in Oklahoma City. He was immediately operated on and, following surgery, remained in critical condition.

********

At one of the next regular staff meetings Sheriff Holcomb introduced David Sable, Pott County's newest deputy. "That raid a couple of weeks ago was really a win-win for us. In addition to getting those dopers out of our county," he explained, "we also got some additional budget from the state to hire one more deputy. This is David Sable, just graduated from the police science program in Oklahoma City." What Sheriff Holcomb did not say, but everyone knew, was that the injuries Dan Morgan sustained would likely keep him out of the field for quite some time – perhaps permanently. The Sheriff's Office could not effectively operate with fewer than seven field officers. No one wanted to think of their office without Deputy Morgan – but each knew it was a real possibility.

"Caleb," Holcomb said following the briefing, "I'd like for you to take Sable under your wing for a couple of weeks. Show him the county; introduce him around – that kind of thing."

As the officers returned to their various assignments, Mary Ellen came over to Caleb and his new charge. "I just got a call from Joe Bob Spangler over on the east side of the county. He's hopping mad – about twenty head have gone missing. He wants somebody out there right away. Sheriff said this'd be a good way to show Deputy Sable what we do." Mary Ellen handed Caleb the pertinent information and turned back to her desk.

On the trip to Spangler's ranch, Caleb updated Sable on the rash of cattle thefts Pott County had been experiencing in recent weeks. Although many people thought rustling was a crime of the old West, it had been reborn as big business in Oklahoma. Stealing cows was relatively uncomplicated and had a big payoff – all a thief needed was a pair of wire cutters and a cattle trailer. With the value of each head at more than $1,000 – rustling was an easy and lucrative way to make illegal bucks. As one of the locals said, "As prices go up, cows go missing."

Although the Oklahoma Department of Agriculture was officially in charge in cases of cattle theft, PottCo residents always called the Sheriff when cows disappeared – "At least the ranchers don't try to track down the thieves and hang them, like in the old days," Caleb noted.

Joe Bob, just as Mary Ellen said, was hopping mad. The two found him near the road just inside his empty catch pen.

"I put twenty head right here in the pen last night," he said just as Caleb and Deputy Sable stepped from their SUV, "because I was going to take them to auction this morning. You know, beef prices are way up now – and I wanted to get them sold. Anyway, I pulled up my trailer this morning – and damned if all of 'em weren't gone. Gone, just gone!"

"Were the cattle branded, Mr. Spangler?" Caleb asked.

"Nope, but they had ear tags – every one of them had an ear tag. What in the hell am I going to do – them cattle was half my profit for this year!"

"Mr. Spangler, this is Deputy Sable. Will you please give him all the details of the theft – as best as you can remember? Like when you put the animals in the pen last night, the description of the cows, the tag numbers – all that. I'll look around and see if I can find anything."

Although Caleb carefully examined the area, he held out little hope he'd find anything helpful. The pattern seemed to be that the rustlers would watch a ranch, learn its routines and when an opportunity presented itself, make off with as many cows as possible. Then the rustlers rushed to get the stolen cattle to auction, sell them off, pocket the profit and go back for another load. Sometimes the rancher didn't even know he'd been robbed until he gathered his herd for auction.

The Oklahoma Cattlemen's Association had strongly encouraged ranchers to brand– and to register those brands. But in practice, most of the ranchers didn't permanently mark each cow. If anything, they used ear tags– and ear tags were easily removed or changed.

Caleb and Sable returned to Shawnee with a laptop full of information – but few clues. They'd do what they could and notify the ODA of Spangler's loss.

It was only two days later, that Caleb and Sable had the chance to interview Joe Bob again - but this time they spoke to him from the local clinic's emergency room. They found Spangler bleeding and bruised, but bristling with righteousness. A nurse was bandaging a superficial gun shot wound to his left arm.

"Those sons-of-bitches come back again. Can you believe it? But I was ready this time. You see, I rounded up another twenty head ready for pickup, and made like I was going to take 'em for auction the next day. But instead of going home that night, my son, my brother and me hid out behind the pen. We brought our rifles with us, too, and it's a damned good thing we did. Those damned Mexicans showed up at midnight with a cattle truck – ready to rip me off again – but we showed 'em. I winged one of 'em at least. Course they got a shot or two off," he looked at his left arm, "- but they didn't get any more of my cattle. They'll think twice about coming back to my place."

Caleb and Sable looked at each other, astonished at the rancher's audacity and relieved Spangler hadn't gotten himself killed.

*********

Jenny spent many of her days refurbishing her treasured home. After she and Caleb married, they'd purchased the old Lovelett place, a turn-of-the century two-story Victorian badly in need of repair. When they first bought it, Jenny and Caleb joked about how they had a lifetime to turn the Lovelett place into the Tallchief mansion – and that it would probably take that long. The house itself stood on a half-acre lot just west of the downtown area – plenty of room for all their animals and the brood of kids they may now never have.

Slowly, the two were restoring the house, but so far they had been able to update only the kitchen and downstairs bathroom. Most of their vacations and free time were spent scraping, painting, hammering and replacing old windows. Their uncommitted resources went to building supplies and labor for a thousand planned and, often unplanned, projects. When they got tired of construction, the twosome would spend Saturdays haunting flee markets or antique stores in search of period building materials or the perfect accessory.

Caleb was worried that the house might turn into a

"money pit," but Jenny loved the old place. She loved the high ceilings, the crown moldings, and the exquisite woodwork. She loved the hidden treasures she found in unexpected places – like the turn-of-the century sewing machine in the attic, or the child's wooden rocking horse in the shed. To Jenny, the house whispered of past loves, happy families and a kinder, more gentle time.

*********

One late blistering hot July afternoon, Sheriff Holcomb called Caleb into his office. Seated across the desk was a woman, probably in her mid-30's, dressed in jeans and a short-sleeved sport shirt. Embroidered on the left side was "Oklahoma Department of Agriculture – Food and Forestry Division." Blonde and a little on the plump side, she conveyed a friendly, but professional no-nonsense attitude. It was not until later Caleb learned she also had a subtle, but extraordinarily well developed sense of humor.

"Agent Amy O'Donnell, this is Undersheriff Tallchief. Caleb, the ODAFF has requested our assistance in apprehending some cattle thieves operating in PottCo."

The ODAFF Agent shook Caleb's hand and leaned back in her chair.

"There was a rash of cattle rustling incidents up in northwest Oklahoma last year," she began. "In three months in just three counties, we had more than a million dollar loss of stock, and the situation's only gotten worse. With the price of beef at an all-time high and the cattle supply at its lowest since the 1950's, the number of thefts has exploded."

She continued, "The thieves, too, aren't your old down-on-their-luck cowboys of yesteryear. They're thugs and they're violent. In Dewey County, one of them shot and wounded a ranch hand that just happened to catch the rustling in progress. The rustlers got away – but at least the rancher didn't lose his herd. Then we had the Spangler incident here in Pottawatomie County last month."

O'Donnell explained, "In the last two weeks we've had five ranch owners in Pottawatomie County report significant losses. The smaller ranchers have been particularly hurt. Twenty head can mean the difference between a marginal profit and bankruptcy. The rustlers must be operating at night and using the back roads, because the highway patrol has been checking all trucks hauling cattle to make sure they had appropriate ownership papers. So far every load has been legitimate."

"We've had agents randomly monitoring some of the larger cattle auctions, checking paperwork and brands, but so far – nothing. The truth of the matter is that the ODA Investigation Division just does not have the staff to keep up with all the thefts. That's why we're asking for some help from you."

**********

After four months, Jenny was physically back to normal. A short pixie-like halo of dark brown hair now framed her face and contrasted even more dramatically with her large blue-grey eyes. Emma thought it gave her an angelic, other-world appearance. Jenny retorted it would take more than a haircut to make her an angel.

The emotional healing, however, had not gone as well. Hurt and fear seemed to reside permanently in Jenny's eyes and actions. It was something Caleb was unaccustomed to seeing. He could feel Jenny distancing herself from him more each day, becoming a little more withdrawn, a little more still, a little more silent. Caleb had done a lot of research about rape victims, and although he somewhat understood Jenny's emotional damage, it still stung him to the core when she pulled away from him or recoiled at his touch. They had tried to make love only once since Jenny's return from the hospital, but the look of terror in Jenny's eyes did more than a cold shower to cool Caleb's ardor. They hadn't tried again.

Most days they politely met each other coming and going, discussed routine daily happenings, but the laughter and the joy were almost gone.

Time, the physicians said, time and counseling would help to make Jenny whole again. Caleb just hoped it was true, because he loved Jenny more than life itself.

**********

Emma returned to the University with strict instructions to finish the new semester. Her financial aid wouldn't tolerate another missed term, and, without it, Emma would never be the second college graduate from the Cochran family. And, a college education was essential to Emma's future, as she was definitely not the type to flip burgers for the rest of her life.

**********

On afternoons Jenny didn't want to work around the house, she and Jesse took long walks together, partly to heal Jenny's body, but more to heal her spirit. They conversed about all things, and Jenny would swear that the big, happy German shepherd understood her better than any other living creature. As she padded along, Jesse would interject just the right chuff or grunt to Jenny's running commentary and she instinctively knew when Jenny needed to rest or share a hug.

"I guess that's not so unusual," Jenny thought. After all, together they had shared moments of terror that had forever changed them both.

On many of those afternoon walks Jenny's thoughts turned to Caleb and their deteriorating relationship. She knew it was her fault, but she didn't seem to be able to do anything about it. Often she would try to recapture her former happiness by recalling more positive times. She frequently thought about her first meeting with Caleb. She was still a student at Oklahoma State and Caleb had been a brand-spanking-new Pottawatomie County deputy.

It was late afternoon on a cold March day when Jenny flew through Caleb's speed trap on Highway 177. She'd been heading home to Stillwater in a vain attempt to see Emma before she went on stage. Emma was starring in her high school senior play and that night was opening night. No way could Jenny miss that – she already had a big bouquet of red roses wrapped up in the back seat, ready for presentation after the play. Jenny was positive Emma's performance would be perfect. Now she was being stopped by this idiot cop.

Deputy Caleb Tallchief, resplendent in his new uniform and sunglasses - the sunglasses were really not necessary this grey afternoon, but they looked so cool - flipped on his lights and gave chase. Jenny saw the lights and vehemently cursed her luck. She veered over to the shoulder, and impatiently drummed her fingers on the steering wheel while she watched the clock tick the minutes away.

Full of authority and himself, the rookie deputy sauntered up to the driver's side of Jenny's beat-up

Hyundai and asked for license and registration. Jenny conjured up a look of false remorse and explained she was hurrying home for a very important occasion. All the while she was thinking "Hurry up, man, and give me that damn ticket. I've got to go."

Caleb looked into Jenny's deep blue-grey eyes and his bravado vanished. He knew he could never give this woman a ticket – he could never purposely do anything to cause her even one bad moment. He was completely lost from the instant he set eyes on her. Caleb stammered a few words about "slowing it down" and let her go. "Forget the warning ticket," he thought to himself, "this woman has places to be."

Jenny carefully pulled back on to the highway, slowly accelerating to the legal speed limit - at least until she was out of sight. Caleb, dazed, walked stiffly back to his patrol car and stood motionless at its door. He stared at Jenny's taillights until they disappeared over the horizon. In that moment, Caleb knew Jenny was *the* one, and he just had to figure out how he could meet her again.

Using conventional and some not-so-conventional resources, Caleb did a little research about this woman who had stolen his heart so easily. He learned her parents had died a few years earlier and that she was now raising her kid sister. He found out she was nearing the end of her degree program in vet med at Oklahoma State University, and, as most vet med seniors, was looking for internship opportunities. It just so happened that Caleb knew an excellent vet in his home town of Tecumseh, and one that could probably be persuaded to take on an intern as fine as Jennifer Lynn Cochran.

It didn't take much convincing to have Doc call the Veterinary Internship Coordinator at OSU. The coordinator turned out to be an old professional friend of Doc's and, to Caleb's relief, recommended Jenny wholeheartedly. Doc offered Jenny the position and she accepted.

And the rest, as they say, was history.

\*\*\*\*\*\*\*\*\*\*

The foursome standing around the coffee pot in the Sheriff's break room erupted in laughter at the story Amy O'Donnell told about one of her cases in Woodward County.

"….and the wife charged up to the auctioneer and started whaling on her – yelling, 'You stupid cunt – you can't get away with sleeping with my husband and then charging double the auction fee!' It took three big, burly men to pull her off the podium."

In recent weeks, Agent O'Donnell had become "one of the boys." She spent considerable time at the Shawnee office as she and the Pottawatomie law enforcement officers concentrated their investigative efforts on the recent rash of cattle thefts. The men, and even Mary Ellen Moore, had come to like and respect the witty and intelligent ODAFF agent. She was good at what she did. She knew it and didn't have to prove it.

The Sheriff had also allocated considerable departmental resource to the cattle rustlings; set up surveillance teams, road blocks, and canvassed cattle auctions. So far, the strategies employed by his men or the ODAFF had yielded nothing. It seemed that no matter where the deputies were in the county – it was the wrong place or the wrong time. The score continued at cattle rustlers 100%; law enforcement zero.

Sheriff Holcomb swiped at the tears of laughter rolling down his cheeks and turned away toward Caleb. "Who's got the southeast corner tonight?" he asked, referring to the night's surveillance assignment.

"Sable," Caleb answered. "O'Donnell and I are going to take the northwest section. Neither of those quadrants has been hit in a couple of weeks – they're due. Mary Ellen has the whole week's schedule, if you want it."

Much later that evening, Caleb and Amy sat in the quiet watching one of the county's larger ranches, but it wasn't a ranch in the northwest quadrant. At the last minute, the two had decided to stake out a property nearer Shawnee. As they were leaving the office, Mary Ellen Moore mentioned that one of her church members was planning to take his herd up to auction the next day. The partners decided to take a serendipitous chance the rustlers also knew of the rancher's plans and would act.

Mary Ellen's intelligence was right on the mark, as always. The rancher's cattle had already been herded into the roadside catch pen. It was the perfect opportunity for the cattle rustlers to score big.

The two found a perfect surveillance position above the road and settled in to wait. The night air was heavy with an impending storm. The cattle in the catch pen paced nervously. To pass the time, Caleb and Amy talked of anything and everything. O'Donnell relayed some additional funny, and sometimes sad, adventures she'd had as an ODAFF agent. Caleb responded with his own tales from the Sheriff's Office. Later O'Donnell reminisced about her failed marriage, and her father's failing health.

Suddenly and directly above their vehicle, a tremendous shaft of lightning split the sky. Instantaneously, thunder crashed and the landscape quaked. Amy jumped straight up and grabbed Caleb's hand. She quickly pulled it back, but Caleb's hand burned where her fingers had touched.

Amy blurted, "You know, I never get used to how fast these summer storms break – or how loud they are." The sky unleashed a torrent of rain, blanketing their SUV and obscuring the landscape in liquid motion. It was almost as if some unseen god had sliced open the underbelly of the black clouds above, allowing the rain to tumble down like a waterfall. Between the booms of thunder, one could almost hear the raindrops sizzle as they hit the overheated earth. After five minutes or so, the storm abruptly stopped just as suddenly as it had begun.

"Well, that was hardly enough to settle the dust," commented Caleb. Then he sat straight up and exclaimed, "Oh shit! "I haven't told the office that we changed our surveillance location." Caleb picked up his mic and relayed the new site to dispatch.

A moment later, O'Donnell whispered, "Caleb, do you see that?" Amy gestured towards the road below. Out of the gloom, a pair of headlights appeared. They were attached to a pickup truck, pulling a large cattle trailer. The color of the pickup was impossible to determine in the dark, but the trailer was large enough to hold the number of cows held in the catch pen. The truck slowed almost to a stop as it approached the enclosure.

The two officers inside the SUV exchanged wide, satisfied smiles; sure they had finally caught a break.

But just as Caleb reached for the police radio to call for backup, the truck sped up and continued down the road toward the highway. Caleb and Amy looked questioningly at each other.

"What was that all about?" asked Amy. Then, "Let's follow and at least get tag numbers. We probably don't want to stop them. We don't want to alert anyone we have the ranches under surveillance just yet."

Caleb nodded his agreement and started the engine.

# Chapter 4

That September Jenny went back to work part-time. Interaction with Doc was almost the same; perhaps he was just slightly less acerbic. Doc and Jenny agreed that – at least for now - she should be less visible to the clients of the Clinic than she'd been before. For the most part, the people in and around Tecumseh were kind folks, but they were, after all, people. Everyone knew what had happened to her at the hands of the convicts and many were anxious to talk to her personally and find out all the lurid details. Others just wanted to see the little woman who had blown away Harlan Ray Lucas. So, instead of meeting personally with the Clinic's patrons, Jenny took over most of the surgery responsibilities. She handled the drop-off patients (those who left their pets in the morning to be picked up in the afternoon), and took a couple of on-line continuing education classes.

When Jenny finally felt up to meeting with clients, Doc and Annie selected those who would be more sensitive to Jenny's emotional state. Doc handled the rubber-neckers.

By October most routines returned to the way they were before Jenny and Jesse were injured. There was one exception - Doc never left Jenny alone. When he visited local farms and ranches, he made sure Jenny went along.

Before the attack Jenny had shied away from the big animals as much as she could get away with. Her petite size made ministering to them difficult and physically challenging. The horses especially seemed to take pleasure in shoving her around.

That no longer appeared to be the case. Even Doc, stingy with compliments, commented on Jenny's new-found skill in working with the behemoths. Jenny, too, was happy and a little surprised. She felt she was finally beginning to understand their needs with the intuition all good vets have.

Her diagnostic skills had become almost too good to be true. At first Jenny chalked up her successes to intuition and deduction based on the animal's symptoms. But lately, it was as if the ailing animal was able to tell Jenny where it hurt. Local patrons began asking for Dr. Tallchief when bringing their pets into the Clinic, rather than grudgingly accepting her as a second-best when the real "Doc" was not around.

Late one afternoon, Annie stuck her head in the all-purpose workroom, which also substituted as Jenny's office. "You won't believe this," she said, "but Miss

Miller and Sissy want to see you. Not Doc – you." Since the incident with the two convicts last spring, Miss Miller would only bring her precious Sissy to see Doc.

"You've got to be kidding," said Jenny, rising from her seat behind the worktable. "Okay, let's see what this is about."

Naomi Miller was nervously pacing inside Examination Room 1. "Oh Dr. Tallchief, I just don't know what to do," she wrung her hands. "Sissy just won't eat and she just lies around with no energy at all. I know cats sleep a lot – but sometimes I can't even get Sissy to eat her favorite treat. Doc has looked at her three times and can't find anything wrong with her. But she keeps getting worse. Do you think she's dying?"

Jenny took in the elderly lady's agitation and feeling her usual exasperation, said, "Well, I doubt Sissy is dying, Ms. Miller. Let's look at her."

When Jenny lifted the large Siamese out of its travel crate, she sensed that the cat was a little nauseous and totally irritated with her owner. "Has Sissy eaten anything new lately – new food- maybe she picked up something from outside. Have you changed her routine in any way?"

"No, no. Doc asked me the same thing. I'm feeding her the same cat food I've always fed her. It's that special diet that we buy right here. Nothing's different." Naomi's hands flew to her mouth, "Do you think some hateful person *poisoned* my precious baby?"

Jenny stroked the animal's light-colored fur. She got the image of Naomi forcing a spoonful of something down Sissy's throat. "Now where did that come from?" she thought to herself.

"Miss Miller, have you been giving Sissy any kind of special vitamins or medicine - anything like that - lately?"

"Well," Naomi turned pink, "as a matter of fact, yes," she replied sheepishly. "I didn't mention this to Doc, but Mother had this wonderful vitamin mixture. She made us take it every day without fail from the time we were children, and she took it herself. I still take it, too, every day. It tastes awful, but Mother swore it would keep a person fit and give you a long, healthy life. It works, too. You know Mother just recently passed – and she was 102."

Naomi sighed, "I thought it would be good for Sissy, too," she said, hanging her head. "I just couldn't bear to lose my baby – I wanted to make sure she'd live a very long time – like Mother did."

But instead of chastising Naomi for force feeding her cat an untried concoction, Jenny recalled a conversation she and Caleb had one evening. Jenny had been complaining about Sissy and Naomi Miller.

Naomi, Caleb had said, was a sad old maid who'd always lived with her mother. The elderly Mrs. Miller was the town's matriarch, dictating in minutia the lives of her children, nieces, nephews, servants, and anyone else unlucky enough to fall within her sphere of influence. Naomi, he'd continued, had lived under her mother's thumb all her life. He doubted the woman had ever made a decision on her own - except once. The one and only time Naomi stood up to her mother was when she bought Sissy – Mrs. Miller wanted her daughter to get rid of the cat. Naomi absolutely refused and, unbelievably, made it stick. Sissy – well, Sissy became the child Naomi never had. Jenny should cut the woman some slack.

"Now," Jenny thought to herself, "Naomi has nobody – except for Sissy. No wonder she's afraid of losing her cat."

Jenny put her arm around the old woman's shoulders and said, "You know, Miss Miller – most people don't know it, but the food you buy here has all the special cat vitamins and minerals Sissy needs. Although vitamins are generally a very good idea, Sissy's probably just getting too many with the extra spoonful you're giving her. I think if you stop giving Sissy your mother's mixture, she'll probably get back to her normal self. And, if you want me to, I'll be happy to check her out as often as you wish at no charge – that way we can make sure Sissy is just fine without the extra dosage."

"Oh thank you, Dr. Tallchief, thank you." Jenny handed Naomi a tissue to wipe her eyes and blow her nose. "You know, my cousin Marvin told me you'd really hit the nail on the head with the treatment you prescribed for his hunting dog. He said nobody else had been able to figure out what was wrong. He was so right. You are a miracle worker. I'll stop giving Sissy the spoonful of vitamins right away."

Miss Miller bustled Sissy back into her crate, picked it up, and turned to leave the room. At the door she actually gave Jenny a tearful smile. "I'll let you know how she is, Doctor, and I'll be sure to check with you before giving Sissy anything else extra."

"Now that was weird – how *did* I know Naomi was giving Sissy something that was making the cat sick?" Jenny thought to herself. She held her hands up to her eyes and carefully examined them, turning them over and over. "What's going on here?"

And the Sissy episode was not the only one. About two weeks later Doc received an emergency call to go out to Taylor's Ranch, about five miles out of town. He took Jenny along.

The Taylors had lived in the area for many years - the 1000-acre ranch handed down from generation to generation. The Taylors ran cattle for the most part. Bill Taylor, Sr. had a champion Angus bull named Lancaster – and Lancaster was his pride and joy. He put the bull out to stud – a win-win situation for himself and Lancaster. Lately, however, Taylor told Doc, the bull had been as disinterested in love-making as he was in eating. His overall behavior had been erratic and unpredictable. Bill, Sr. was a worried man.

Jenny followed Doc to the 50' x 25' pen holding the bull. The animal ceaselessly paced the perimeter fence – back and forth – back and forth.

Doc instructed Jenny to remain outside the pen while he and Bill went in. As the two men approached the 2000 pound animal, Lancaster suddenly bellowed, turned and charged straight towards them. He knocked Doc to the ground as he sped by, heading hell-bent for Jenny. Before she could react, the bull had pushed his nose and part of his head through the opening between the slats.

Instinctively, Jenny threw up her hands to shield herself and momentarily touched the head of the rampaging animal. Immediately, she got a mental image of a large mountain lion. She also sensed the bull was deeply afraid.

All of this information was relayed to her in the split second it took for the bull to pull back into the pen. The men, with the help of Bill's eldest two sons, finally got the big animal sedated.

"See Doc, this is the kind of thing Lancaster's been pullin' for the last week. I don't know what to do with him."

Doc examined the bull, but could detect nothing on the surface that would explain his bizarre behavior.

"I'm going to take some samples, Bill, and run some tests. We'll see what we can see."

Jenny had moved up beside Doc. When Bill headed over to the barn, she said, "You know, Doc, I was thinking. Maybe Lancaster's just plain scared. Has there been any mountain lion or coyote activity around here?"

"Well, I don't know, but it's a good question." Doc called out, "Hey, Bill, you had any trouble with mountain lions, coyotes around here lately?"

"Nope."

"Well, okay. I'll let you know the test results as soon as I can."

Later that afternoon, Doc received an email from Bill Taylor. It read:

> Doc, after you mentioned the mountain lion idea, I put out a note on the PottCo rancher's list serve. Sure enough, the MacKays about ten miles east of us have had some run-ins with a huge mountain lion. It disappeared about two weeks ago. The boys and I checked out the perimeter around the far pasture where Lancaster grazes and guess what, we found spoor. We'll take it from here. Thanks, Doc. You're the best.
>
> Bill Taylor

# Chapter 5

A picture-perfect autumn sky framed the brilliant hues of the oak, elm and pine lining the roadway. "Almost like a postcard," Caleb Tallchief thought as he leisurely drove his patrol SUV down the section line near Hubble's ranch. Although Caleb was officially looking for any suspicious cattle theft activity, he was generally just enjoying the tranquility of the lovely autumn day.

Even the dust churned up by Caleb's passage was mellow this afternoon. It marked his passing but remained low to the ground and settled back comfortably to earth. Most years, the lack of rain and the high temperatures of late summer condemned all the trees around these parts to a drab funeral. The dust choked most horses – not to mention the people.

But not this fall. The unusually wet summer had left a legacy of beautiful red, orange, green and yellow color. "Pretty soon all the old geezers will be out in force - taking bus tours all along the Talihina Drive, gawking at all the trees. Heaven help us," Caleb thought. Then he smiled, "hopefully, Jenny and I will survive this to be one of those old geezer couples someday."

As Caleb's mind drifted along, going nowhere, a blur of dark brown fur streaked across the road in front of him. Caleb slammed on his brakes, but heard a sickening "thud" as he hit the Springer spaniel, going hell-bent for who-knows-where.

"Oh, shit." Caleb scrambled out of the SUV to find the limp body of the large dog where he'd landed in the far borrow ditch. The dog's eyes looked sadly at Caleb, as if to accuse him of careless driving.

"Look, you're the one who darted out in front of me.….not the other way 'round…" He paused. "Why am I explaining this to a dog?"

Caleb didn't recognize the animal and the vaccination tag named an Oklahoma City vet. Jenny would just have to track it down once he took the dog into the clinic.

"Ok fella," Caleb softly continued, as he gently lifted the animal and placed him in the back of the truck, "I know a really great vet who will fix you right up. Don't you worry about anything." He doubled up the small blanket stashed under the seat and rested the dog's head on it.

As Caleb turned the truck toward the clinic, he picked up his cell phone and called Jenny at home. She answered on the second ring.

"Hi, honey. Look, I've hit a Springer spaniel out

here by Hubble's, and I'm bringing him into the clinic. He doesn't seem to be hurt very bad, at least I don't see any blood. Can you meet me there? I've promised him the best vet in Oklahoma, so I can't possibly leave him in the hands of Doc."

Jenny laughed.

"Damn, it was good to hear that," thought Caleb.

"Sure, Caleb. Or should I call you Crash? I'll meet you there."

**********

Caleb took the dirt and gravel roads and turns gently and slowly to keep from jarring the dog any more than necessary. By the time he reached the clinic, his wife was already there.

Jesse, who never seemed to leave Jenny's side these days, began checking out the new patient as soon as Caleb opened the back of the SUV, alternately sniffing, wagging, and circling Caleb as he carried the 85 pound dog inside.

As Caleb eased the injured animal on the examining table, Jesse placed her front paws on the stool next to the patient, bringing her nose-to-nose with the new arrival.

Jenny shooed the shepherd away, "Jesse, how can I help with your big head in the way? Com'on, you know better."

Jesse looked appropriately miffed as she strolled over to the corner and flopped down in her usual place by the radiator. Caleb pulled a stool over beside Jesse, sat down and began to scratch her ears.

"Guess we'd better stay out of the way if we know what's good for us, girl." Jesse chuff'ed her agreement.

Jenny gently placed her hands on the spaniel. Instantly, as if she had just received an electric shock, the image of a small, blonde girl, about three or four years old, flashed across her mind. Jenny jumped back a half-step as Jesse came to her feet and went to her side.

The injured dog lifted his head so that his eyes met Jenny's as if to say, "this is an important thing for you to know.... do something.... help us."

"What's wrong...Jenny?"

"Nothing....I... uh...nothing."

Jenny touched the brown fur once more. Again, the picture flashed in her mind, but this time she could see the child was hurt and crying. Jenny kept her hands in place and the scene expanded, showing the side of a deep ravine with the little girl caught on a slight outcropping about ten feet below the crest. Below her was a drop of more than 100 feet into a small stream at the foot of the cliff face. Somehow, Jenny knew this place was close. But where was it?

Jenny turned her head to meet the deep brown eyes of her patient. Instinctively, she knew the dog had been with the little girl, that somehow the child had fallen, and that the dog had been hit by Caleb's SUV while going for help.

"Caleb, where exactly did you hit the dog?"

"I don't know Jenny, I tried to miss it. I think it was in the hind quarters – maybe back leg."

"No, no, I mean where – location…. where were you driving?"

"Out by Hubble's…"

"Do you know of a sheer cliff face that drops about 100 feet to a small stream around the Hubble place?"

Caleb's forehead furrowed in thought. After half a minute, he responded, "Uh, yeah…. it's on the other side of the section line from Hubble's about, oh maybe 50 – 75 yards before you get to his place and behind a large stand of trees. You can't see it from the road and you have to skirt around a big rock formation to get to it. I haven't been there since I was a little kid. I remember my dad blistered my behind for fooling around there, because it was so dangerous."

"Caleb, you're going to think I have gone completely off my rocker. But I want you to do as I ask – with no questions, OK?"

Caleb looked bewildered, but Jesse began to wag her tail rapid fire. Jenny continued, "Take Jesse, and go look over the cliff face you remember and see if you can find a little girl about 10 feet down on a small outcrop. Please, Caleb, go fast. I think she may be in serious trouble."

Caleb looked into Jenny's eyes and saw that she was deadly serious. Without a word, he pulled his keys from his belt and headed out the door with Jesse on his heels.

In no more than two minutes, Jenny heard the SUV's engine turn over and the tires fight to gain footing in the dirt and gravel outside. Finally, it sped away.

Jenny spoke softly to the large, brown and white dog lying on the table. "Don't you worry. Caleb will find your little girl and bring her home safely."

As if he understood Jenny's words, the spaniel relaxed and closed his eyes, while Jenny made him well.

**\*\*\*\*\*\*\*\*\*\***

Caleb's mind raced faster than the SUV he drove. None of the extensive reading he had done regarding post-traumatic stress disorder, rape crisis intervention or anything else had prepared him for this.

Jenny's wild request – was she losing her reason- her sanity? "Please God, no," he pled aloud.

At one point he slowed almost to a stop, thinking he would turn around and go directly to see Jenny's counselor. Surely, this dumb-ass wild-goose chase was a sign that Jenny's emotional condition was deteriorating.

As Caleb eased the vehicle to the shoulder to stop,

Jesse came to attention in her seat. She gazed directly at Caleb and let go with several rapid-fire barks as if to say, "Hey bud, you promised you'd go look. Get with it, and hurry up."

Caleb returned her stare and relented. "All right… *all right*. I guess I've pissed off enough dogs for today. I'll look – *then* I'll call Jenny's doctor."

**********

Caleb couldn't remember where he should leave the road to find the cliff face. It had been just too many years ago. He thought it was somewhere close to the turn in the road before you hit the Hubble place, but not exactly where. He finally just picked a spot, pulled the SUV over, locked it and headed into the thicket.

Seeming to stumble and catch his pants leg on every step, Caleb thought, "I've got to be out of my mind… given directions by a woman who is obviously mental and two dogs. Maybe I'm the one who's mental." A large branch slipped out of his hand and slapped him right in the face as if to emphasize his stupidity.

Suddenly, Caleb broke through the trees and underbrush and ran smack into the side of the rock formation he remembered from so many years ago. Jesse appeared beside him without a hair out of place. She started to whimper and pull Caleb's pant leg in the direction of the cliff face. "Okay, okay, girl. Hold it or you'll send me over."

As Caleb stood at the edge of the drop, he could see nothing. Twilight had darkened the ravine's countenance, making it impossible to see anything clearly. Caleb became perfectly still, holding his breath, but could hear nothing. Even the woods were preternaturally silent.

After a long moment, he patted Jesse on the head and said sadly, "Come on, girl. Let's go." Although Caleb knew in his mind this was a fool's errand, his heart nonetheless wanted to believe Jenny hadn't been fantasizing.

Jesse would not go. She pointedly sat down and cocked her head to the side as if to say, "Listen. I hear something." Caleb squatted down beside the still dog and willed himself to be silent. After a long moment, a very small voice, almost a whisper, drifted up to his ears. "...itsy, itsy 'pider went to water 'pout....down down rain and 'pider went...out."

"Oh, my God," he thought. Caleb carefully lowered himself to the ground and inched out as far as he could. There to his right about fifteen feet below in a dark enclave of rock and earth was the source of the whimsical, melody-free song.

A small dirt-streaked angelic face surrounded by a halo of platinum white hair looked up at him and smiled. Her face was barely illuminated by the fading evening light– her fingers poised to play "Itsy-bitsy spider."

Caleb's heart was racing. "Softly, calmly- don't scare her," Caleb cautioned himself.

"Hi. I'm Caleb. What's your name?"

"Lindsey Ann. I fall down."

"I can see you did. Are you hurt?"

"Uh huh." Head nods.

"Can you see me?"

"Uh huh."

Suddenly, tears welled up in her eyes, "I want my mommy." Her lips began to quiver.

"Okay, sweetheart. Listen to me. I'm a policeman and I'm going to get you out of there. But you have to stay very still and not move. Can you do that?"

"Uh huh."

"Can you see Jesse dog?" Jesse scooted on her belly out to the edge of the overhang, hung her head over the side and woofed softly.

"Uh huh"

"Okay, I have to go get a rope so I can come down there to get you. Jesse will stay here with you, but it's real important that you don't try to move, OK?"

"Uh huh." Big nod of the little head.

Caleb turned to the dog. "Jesse, stay. I'll be right back."

Caleb ran as fast as he could back through the brush with his hands shielding his face, ignoring the sting of the stickers and the slap of the branches.

As he ran, one thought played and replayed itself over and over in his mind. "Oh, my God…oh, my God. How in the hell did Jenny know? How in the hell did Jenny know?"

\*\*\*\*\*\*\*\*\*\*

When Caleb returned to the cliff face with the rope and flashlight, he checked on Lindsay. "Ok, Lindsay, I'm back. I'm coming to get you right now."

Jesse was exactly where he had left her; she didn't take her eyes off the child even as Caleb made ready to descend the cliff face.

After securing the line's end around a heavy-duty oak, Caleb carefully lowered himself to Lindsey's perch. He pulled her to his chest and told her to 'hug his neck tight,' although it soon became apparent Lindsay needed no instructions. Her strangle-hold around Caleb's neck almost cut off his air supply.

Her 'hurts' turned out to be scratches and bruises and possibly a broken leg – "nothing too serious, please God," he thought. Caleb carried her back to the SUV like the precious gift she was and wrapped her in a blanket.

Jesse jumped in the back seat, but stuck her head between Caleb and Lindsay so as not to be left out of the action. Lindsay giggled.

When he had the child settled comfortably and seat-belted in, Caleb called Jenny. He wasn't sure what to say, so he just stuck to the facts.

"Jenny, I found the little girl. She's fine. I....I don't know what else to say. She was right where you said she'd be."

Silence on the other end of the line.

"Jenny, are you there?"

"Yes, Caleb. I'm here. Look, you can't say how this happened....I ...I don't know what happened and I sure couldn't explain it to anyone else right now. OK?"

"But how...."

"Just say the dog led you to her – I mean, that's really true, isn't it? You're just leaving out what happened in the middle. Just say you hit the dog, but he still led you to the little girl...."

"I guess I can make that believable..."

"Please, Caleb . I need time to figure this out ..."

"Okay, sweetheart. I ran over the dog, but he was still able to show me where the little girl was. That's my story and I'm sticking to it."

"Thanks, Caleb. I really do love you, you know."

Caleb's heart soared. It had been many months since Jenny had said anything like this. "Jenny, I love you, too."

Caleb started the car and headed for the hospital. As he hit the blacktop, his next call was to the dispatcher.

Mary Ellen's high-pitched voice immediately blared back at him. "Caleb where have you....

"Mary Ellen, hush up and listen. I'm bringing a

little girl named Lindsay Ann Young to County. She looks to be about three or four. She fell down a steep cliff over near Hubble's place. I think she may have a broken leg, but otherwise she seems to be okay."

"*Thank the Lord.* Emil Hubble just called in - frantic. His granddaughter, Lindsay, you know, Sarah's youngest, has gone missing. They're having some kind of family reunion over at his place and she wandered off. I'll call them and tell 'em to meet you at County. Praise the Lord."

Caleb grinned. No matter how many times Mary Ellen had been cautioned about using proper police jargon and omitting the religious references when transmitting, she simply refused to comply. Every time the Sheriff broached the subject, she would just give him one of those, "you can talk 'til you're blue in the face, but I'm going to do it my way," looks and proceed as usual. She knew her job was safe.

And she was right, too. No one, especially the Sheriff, could imagine the Sheriff's Office without Mary Ellen. She knew everything about everybody. Her church network was better than twenty undercover cops. If the Sheriff had been forced to choose which of his officers was the most efficient in preventing or solving crimes in his county, he'd have been hard pressed not to name Mary Ellen Moore.

Caleb turned to Lindsay.

"Lindsay, is your grandpa's name Emil Hubble?"

"Huh-uh. It's papa."

Caleb smiled. It had to be the lost child. After all, how many children can go missing in one afternoon out here?

"Well, your mommy and daddy and papa and grandma are on their way to the hospital to pick you up right now. How about if we turn on the siren and all the lights?"

"Yeah!"

# Chapter 6

Caleb surveyed the scene from atop the red, white and blue crepe paper-decorated platform, inhaling the crisp October air. Flags snapped in the breeze as one or two of the less-well anchored streamers escaped their bondage. The high school band tuned up for a stirring rendition of the Star-Spangled Banner.

Merle Jennings, cursing softly, jiggled wires under the podium in a vain attempt to get the microphones to stop those irritating high-pitched squeals.

Mayor Lester Martin, Doc's brother, practiced his glad-handing techniques just in front of the stand. Those spectators on the front row jealously guarded their spots, while latecomers jockeyed for a better view. Kids were hoisted on parent's shoulders.

It was a beautiful Indian summer afternoon, and the citizens of Tecumseh had reason to celebrate. After all, it wasn't every day a town could honor real-live heroes – and hometown heroes at that

Sharing the spotlight today was Scooter, the Springer spaniel. Actually, the dog was more the focus of attention than the Undersheriff. "That's probably because I turned him into Superdog with my story," thought Caleb sarcastically.

Caleb had kept his word to Jenny. He told the Sheriff and the press that Scooter, after being hit by his SUV, led Caleb to the side of the ravine and to Lindsay. And, the dog did so with a broken leg.

Nobody ever put it together that the dog with him at County was Jesse, not Scooter. And when Scooter later emerged from the vet clinic complete with leg cast, the media went wild. The story had even made national news. "It *really* must have been a slow news day," Caleb thought.

Although Caleb had feared Lindsay Ann might have had a broken leg, it turned out to be just a sprain. Within a few days, the four-year-old was back to playing at full-speed, equipped with a whole series of new stories to impress her fellow preschoolers.

"Sometimes life is very good," Caleb reminded himself.

Caleb glanced at Jenny sitting on his left, instinctively reaching for her hand. Thank God he stopped before she noticed. She was already nervous enough with all these people around. Jenny was struggling with any human contact right now and, for better or worse, the people in this town were 'huggers.' Especially today, everybody wanted to pat his back, shake his hand or both at the same time. When they couldn't get to Caleb, Jenny was the next-best thing. She was a real trooper, he thought, looking at her bright smile. No one would ever know.

Another thing no one in the town would ever know is that Jenny had been the real hero.

Caleb was jolted from his reverie by the sound of tires skidding to a stop just outside the cordoned-off platform area. Caleb looked over to see State Senator Charlie Bishop, 'the ranchers' friend,' stepping down pretentiously from the driver's side of his black Ford 250 pickup. Slightly rotund and well-tanned, Charlie Bishop's persona was, as always, the perfect archetype of the rural Oklahoma farmer or rancher. He wore his sweat-stained light grey Stetson pushed back on his forehead, and his jacket carried the PottCo Cattlemen's Association logo. Charlie took off his hat and waved it to the crowd.

"I should have known," thought Caleb, "no way would that son-of-a-bitch miss a chance to gain political capital – especially in an election year." He watched the long-time politician smoothly work the crowd as he made his way toward the platform.

Sheriff Holcomb was livid. He leaned over and whispered to Caleb, "That sorry glory-seeking shit – you might have known he'd show up." Sheriff Holcomb detested the senator. To Holcomb, Charlie Bishop represented the very worst in Oklahoma rural politics.

Charlie Bishop had been representing the district for more than 25 years – actually – he'd been at the state capitol for more than 25 years. Holcomb was not sure whether he'd represented any of his constituents' interests or just his own personal ambitions. During his time in office, Bishop had managed to wheedle or bribe himself into almost every enterprise in the county. He knew everyone and owned many of them.

Sheriff Joseph Holcomb was one of the exceptions. He was a completely honest man. Though Senator Bishop had supported Holcomb's first successful election campaign, the 'quid pro quo' exchange Bishop expected in return never materialized. Holcomb would not 'fix' things when a 'fix' was suggested by Bishop's people. Special favors were never requested by the senator personally, nor would it have made any difference if they were.

In the last election, the Bishop political machine supported Holcomb's opponent – and the Sheriff had won by only the smallest of margins. Caleb knew that should Bishop's candidate of choice ever be elected sheriff, he'd be out of a job. But that was just fine with him – no way would Caleb ever work for a Bishop flunkey.

The Mayor scrambled to find a seat for the senator. He didn't see anyone on the dais he could unobtrusively kick off to make room for their prominent but unexpected guest so he quickly sent Merle Jennings to the corner "Beer & Cheer." Jennings hurried back with a somewhat scarred wooden barrel chair – not exactly the seating the Mayor had in mind – but it would have to do.

In the end it did not really matter. When gaining the platform, Bishop went immediately to the microphone and waved his hands pontifically over the crowd, commanding silence.

"Friends, what a wonderful day here in Tecumseh. And what better way to spend it than to honor our own home-town heroes." He gestured vaguely in the direction of Caleb and Scooter, never breaking eye contact with his audience. The crowd roared.

"I was so pleased to be invited to be a small part of this joyous celebration. You know I am so proud to be a member of this great community." More applause.

"Sorry to say I can only stay a minute, but there're several bills in the senate right now that affect all of us greatly – especially you - our fine Pottawatomie ranchers and farmers. I need to hurry back there to make sure your interests are heard. But I couldn't miss this chance to say 'Well done to my friends in the Sheriff's Office. Thank you again for including me and God bless you all." He basked in the applause for a minute, and then turned, tipped his hat to the ladies on the stage, returned to his vehicle, waved once more for the crowd, and was gone. "Like a thief in the night," thought Caleb sarcastically.

Once the people had returned their collective attention to the podium, the Mayor, slightly flustered, said, "Well – well, that was quite a surprise. What an honor to have Senator Bishop here to say a few words."

Holcomb squirmed in his seat. "But now folks, let's hear from the hero himself - our own Caleb Tallchief."

Stepping up to the podium, Caleb looked over the crowd at people he had known all his life. Mary Ellen Moore was right there up front; just beaming dressed in her Sunday best, waving her embroidered handkerchief at Caleb and Jenny. After all, Caleb *was* one of hers. Emma, too, had driven down for the weekend to bask in the celebrity status of her brother-in-law. He could see her off to the left, flirting with Matt, his susceptible younger brother. Neither Matt nor Emma was paying any attention to what was happening on stage.

Many of the town's people called Matt and Caleb salt and pepper. They were just two years apart in age - both about the same size, tall, well built and had a quiet strength about them. However, where Caleb was blonde and blue-eyed, Matt had dark brown hair and eyes. Both had been high school 'jocks' – Matt in football and Caleb in baseball. Both had been popular and pursued by their female classmates, but where Caleb played the field; Matt dated the same girl exclusively.

Matt's high school love dumped him not long after graduation, and some said Matt hurried to enlist in the army because of a broken heart. Truthfully, Matt signed up because he wanted adventure and travel. His time in the military had provided both. Afghanistan proved to be more adventure than Matt ever wanted. When his enlistment time was up, he was more than ready to come home. Even though Matt's MOS was as a supply officer – and not frontline combat - he'd seen enough tragedy and bloodshed to last him a lifetime.

Matt had shipped home about a month ago. He was currently working at their grandfather's Feed & Seed Store and had been thinking of applying to OU as a business major. For even though war in the far-away deserts of the Middle East was not his 'cup of tea,' Matt had enjoyed the business aspects of his army assignment. Now he had the GI Bill to help pay for his college costs, and his grandfather encouraged him to apply for one or more of the lucrative Native American grants, too. Matt was still considering his options.

Back on the platform Caleb blushed as he thanked the City Council for the medal. "You know, this medal should really be made of prime rib and hung around Scooter's neck. He's the real hero of the day. Thanks for including me." The crowd burst into applause and laughter.

When the Mayor at last concluded his wrap-up speech, which was actually more about the Mayor's accomplishments than the two honorees, Caleb was finally able to exit the stage. Jenny followed close on his heels. There was still the bar-b-que picnic later that afternoon at 'The Park' on Park Street, but he and Jenny had decided she could feign a migraine so that she wouldn't be put through that ordeal, too. As they headed for Jenny's five-year old Ford pickup, Emil Hubble caught up with them.

Caleb almost didn't recognize the man because

he was all dressed up in a suit, rather than his usual bib overalls. The ever-present worn straw cowboy hat, however, was a dead give-away.

"Caleb, I can't tell you how grateful I am for you finding our Lindsay. She's such a sweet little thing and the light of her grandmother's eyes. I feel so bad about not keeping better track of her."

"You know, we left her big brother to watch out over her and he got to messing around and …well. Then he went lookin' for her without telling anybody. He spent more'n two hours lookin' for her. I guess he hoped he'd find her before his daddy found out he'd lost her. Been through seven kinds of hell, too, that kid, not counting the whippin' his daddy gave him. Anyway, you can't know how much we are in your debt."

Mr. Hubble's eyes began to tear up. He turned from Caleb and pulled out his handkerchief, loudly blowing his nose. "Damn hay fever," he said. "Anyhow, if there's anything you or yours need; you call me. You hear?"

Caleb shook Emil's hand and patted him on the back, "You know I will, Mr. Hubble."

"And from now on, you call me Emil."

# Chapter 7

The evening was a rollicking success. Caleb's brothers, parents, and grandparents stopped by the house after the city's festivities, and Emma flirted shamelessly with them all.

Where Jenny had always been somewhat quiet and shy, Emma was a natural entertainer. Charismatic and beautiful, Emma's intelligent witticisms kept the evening lively and full of laughter. She could coax smiles from the most stoic, including Caleb's father. Jenny was more relaxed and happy than Caleb had seen her in a very long time.

It was late when the Tallchiefs said their good-byes. Emma, too, finally seemed to run out of steam and headed zombie-like toward the downstairs guestroom. She was unaware that on most nights these days, Jenny slept in that bedroom alone.

Jenny wasn't sure why she started sleeping downstairs. At first, she said it was because she didn't sleep well and didn't want to keep Caleb awake. But the truth was she just felt more relaxed and secure in the small corner room where many of her childhood memories were on display or packed away carefully in her mother's hope chest.

And sleeping with Caleb made her nervous. She was afraid he might want to touch her or make love, and she wasn't sure she could handle that. Caleb never said a word when she began sleeping downstairs, but Jenny knew she had hurt him deeply.

This night, however, Jenny shared Caleb's bed. They talked late into the night about the unexplainable message she'd received from Scooter. Jenny finally told Caleb about the other times she had felt a strange intuitive understanding of an animal's thoughts, including the time she was charged by Taylor's champion bull.

"I don't know what's happening to me, Caleb. It's almost as if I can read animals' minds – but only sometimes – like when the animal is really scared. You don't think I'm going crazy, do you?"

"Of course not, Jen. But something sure is happening. I've heard of people developing psychic abilities after a severe trauma, but that's always been through interaction with other people or objects or seeing the future – that sort of thing. I never heard of anybody communicating with animals – except, of course, Dr. Doolittle."

Caleb's attempt to lighten up the situation fell on deaf ears.

He continued, "Okay, Jenny, maybe it's time to revise

my Neanderthal thinking. If psychic abilities exist, why can't animals communicate that way? They're creatures with feelings and intellect."

"I guess it's possible. But I don't want other people to know what really happened. I'm enough of a freak in this town already. I don't want people to think I'm psycho, too." Jenny turned over and put out the light on her side of the bed.

"Well," Caleb thought sarcastically to himself, "I handled that really well."

Later that night, Caleb awoke to hear Jenny softly crying. He pretended to be asleep, knowing she could not accept either his comfort or his touch.

**********

At breakfast the next morning, a rejuvenated Emma was packed and ready to go. She said she had to get back to the Edmond house she rented with two other students to study for a big biology exam the upcoming Monday. "Why do we have to take all this unnecessary crap? I'm never going to use it. All I really want to do is write screen plays or maybe do some acting."

Her sister commiserated and tried to be encouraging. Theater was Emma's love and drama was her life. What Jenny didn't say was the chances of Emma's becoming a super star were infinitesimal and this "unnecessary crap" would probably be extremely important to her when she was looking for a job that would actually pay the bills. "It's hard to be a sister and a parent," Jenny sighed to herself.

Out in the driveway the two sisters hugged goodbye. Emma got into her ancient red Ford, slammed the door and started the engine. Luckily, it caught on the second try.

Just as Emma began to wave goodbye, Jenny noticed the oversized ring with the letter "E" emblazoned in rhinestones on her right hand. "What's that?"

"Oh, Matt bought this for me at the fair yesterday," Emma said, trying to be nonchalant. "Actually, um," Emma continued, "I'd like to come down the third weekend in November, if that's okay…" her voice softened.

"Sure, you know you're always welcome. Something special, or did you just want to see more of your stogy old sister?"

"Well, actually, um….I have a date with Matt."

Much to Jenny's surprise, Emma actually blushed. "He's taking me to the Vince Gill concert in Fort Smith." And before Jenny could respond, the petite blonde hurriedly put the car in drive and threw a kiss in Jenny's general direction.

"See you soon. I love you guys." trailed off behind her as the dust from the gravel enveloped the rapidly departing vehicle.

"Well, that was interesting," Jenny thought, alarm bells going off in her head. Emma was notorious for breaking hearts, and she hoped Matt's would not be next. What havoc that could reek on the whole family dynamic. "What do you think?" she asked Jesse, as she held open the kitchen's weather-worn screen door.

Jesse rolled her eyes and said nothing.

# Chapter 8

The following weeks slipped into monotony. Caleb continued working all kinds of crazy hours; he and O'Donnell surveilling county ranches and staking out cattle auctions. Jenny and Jesse continued their daily long walks, sometimes silently; sometimes with a running commentary from Jenny.

**********

Unknown to Caleb or Jenny, Matt and Emma began seeing each other – at first occasionally – but lately – two or three times a week. Even though their personalities were very different, they found they liked the same things and thought the same way about an amazing number of issues. And there was enough difference to keep things lively. For instance, they totally disagreed over politics. Both argued intelligently and rationally, and in the end, agreed to disagree.

Emma thought Matt was 'hot.' Matt thought Emma was the most beautiful, intelligent and witty woman he had ever met.

Emma had given Matt a campus tour, hoping he might consider coming to UCO for his business degree – rather than so far away in Norman. This was the first time she could remember feeling 'so right' about anyone she had dated, and it was the first time she had even considered a long-term relationship. Matt, ever the pragmatist, was shopping for engagement rings.

**\*\*\*\*\*\*\*\*\*\***

One afternoon in mid-November, Amy O'Donnell asked Caleb to join her for lunch at Ellie's Deli and Café on Broadway. The restaurant was located on the west side of the street, right in the heart of the downtown district. That is, if one could call a span of three blocks a downtown district. Tecumseh was, like many small towns in Oklahoma, an interesting mix of old, new and repurposed buildings – some dating back to pre land-run days and others new construction. A brand new brick and mortar bank might reside next to a dilapidated boarded-up antique store. Zoning was an unknown concept.

Ellie's was one of the older brick structures that

sported a large spotlessly-clean street-front picture window. A slightly faded green awning spanned its length. In the spring and summer, overflowing pots of flowers and sweet-smelling herbs adorned the entry, but just now the containers stood empty and forlorn. The restaurant did not really include a deli, but Ellie's daughter thought she should include the word in the café's name because it was "catchy" and it rhymed with Ellie. So – Ellie's Deli & Café it became and remained.

On the street just to the right of the entryway, a large erasable sandwich board advertised the 'specials' for the day in bright magic marker colors. The sign was generally rimmed with sketches of flowers, ribbons and doodles – "just to add interest" to Ellie's advertising.

The two law officers ordered 'specials' and found a booth next to the window, where they could watch the gently falling snow.

As Amy pushed her food around its plate, Caleb dug in enthusiastically. The undersheriff had almost finished his meal when, finally, Amy broke the silence. "Caleb, I wanted you to be the first to know I've been offered a really good position with the Department of Agriculture in D.C. If I take it, I have to start right away."

Amy studied Caleb carefully, hoping to read his reaction. Caleb returned her stare with a questioning gaze.

"Well," Amy stammered, "the truth is, Caleb, I care a lot for you, and I think you feel something for me, too.

I just don't know what you feel. If there is any hope for us to have a relationship – a serious relationship – I want to give it a chance. I'll turn down the D.C. job - all you have to do is ask." Amy looked for an answer in Caleb's eyes.

Caleb slowly put his fork down. "Amy," he said at last, "I don't know what to say. You have to know I think you're a beautiful and intelligent woman. I do have feelings for you – feelings that sometimes scare me." For a long time, he stared at his almost-empty plate. "But the truth is – I love Jenny with all my heart and soul. She and I have been going through a rough patch – but I have to believe we'll come out of it." He looked into Amy's eyes, "I never want to lose your friendship – but I could never love anyone else but Jenny."

O'Donnell quietly watched as the snowflakes piled up high on the window sill. She nodded her head sadly, "You're a good man, Caleb Tallchief. I guess that's a big part of why I care for you as I do." Amy stood up, smiled at Caleb, and said "See ya."

Then she left - her lunch untouched.

********

On Friday night of the third weekend in November, Jenny waited for Emma to drive in. Emma's "joie de vivre" always lifted her up. At 10:00 pm Jenny started to get worried. At 11:30 she repeatedly called Emma's cell. Each attempt went directly to voice mail and when Emma hadn't arrived by midnight; Jenny called Caleb.

"Caleb, I'm really worried about Emma. She's never this late without calling. Do you think she's had a wreck or broken down somewhere?"

Caleb, too, was concerned. Even though his sister-in-law was a flake, she was a considerate flake. She had just phoned night before last to confirm that she'd be spending the weekend with them - bubbling with excitement about her date with Matt. Caleb checked all the sources he could think of – dispatcher, hospitals, everyone. He even resorted to calling his brother, but the last time Matt had talked with Emma was the preceding Thursday afternoon.

Caleb called in a favor and got one of the other deputies to cover for him so he could go home to pick up Jenny. Together with Jesse, they back-tracked Emma's normal route from Edmond to Tecumseh - methodically searching all the shoulders, medians, and ditches for a trace of her red beat-up Ford. Nothing.

**********

When they finally arrived at Emma's house in the wee hours of the morning, they banged on the front door until one of Emma's roommates, bedraggled and sleep-worn, answered through the closed door.

"What?"

"I'm Emma Cochran's sister, Jenny. She was supposed to come to our house tonight and she hasn't shown up. I can't find her and I'm really, really worried."

The door opened the width of its chain, and a young woman about Emma's age, peered through the crack. Apparently Jenny and Caleb appeared to be legitimate, because the door closed, followed by the screech of the chain disengaging. Finally, the door opened, and they were invited in.

Mary Castleberry, Emma's roommate, peered at the couple through sleep-deprived red-rimmed eyes.

"I recognized you from the photos in Emma's room," she explained to Caleb, "Please come on in and sit down. Just throw that stuff in the floor." She gestured toward the mound of clean/dirty laundry thrown helter-skelter on all the living room furniture.

She continued through an enormous yawn, "I know that Emma was planning to come to your house this weekend, but we haven't really talked since I left for class early Thursday morning. My schedule is unbelievable this semester," she explained, "I'm trying to graduate this next spring – and working two part-time jobs – so we don't see much of each other."

She paused and thought a moment, "But come to think of it – Emma didn't put out any food or water for her new kitten this morning or even Thursday night. I was sort of peeved that she didn't – and didn't even leave me a note to ask if I would – that's weird." Mary's thoughts wandered away.

Caleb asked if he could make some coffee in the hope some caffeine would bring Mary back to earth. She nodded and gestured vaguely in the direction of the kitchen – her attention focused elsewhere.

In contrast to the living room's chaos, the kitchen was exceptionally clean and organized. Only the trash can overflowed with fast food containers and wrappings. Caleb had no trouble at all finding all the makings for a really strong brew. "Obviously," he thought sarcastically, "they eat out a lot."

As Jenny and Mary sat silently opposite one another in the living room, each lost in her own thoughts, Jesse sauntered down the hall into Emma's room. Perched on a pillow at the head of an unmade bed, amidst books, papers, a small laptop, a TV remote and several more fast-food wrappers, was a small, grey and white tailless male kitten – about ten weeks old.

Strangely, the kitten didn't hiss or attempt a leap to safety on top of the nearby armoire as the large dog slipped into the room. Still and alert, his enormous green eyes carefully followed the path of the intruder, watching closely as Jesse sat down just inside the doorway.

After a few moments the kitten jumped from Emma's bed onto the floor, walked around for a bit, and finally settled down on a buff-colored flyer that had apparently slipped from the nightstand. The paper crunched loudly in the silence of the room, as the kitten settled down. Then the two animals stared at one another, neither moving nor making a sound.

Caleb juggled the three steaming mugs of coffee into the living room and went back for milk and sugar. He found some reasonably recent milk in the refrigerator and some packets of sugar substitute. By the time he returned to the living room, the aroma of the coffee seemed to be doing its magic. Both Jenny and Mary seemed to be more alert and focused. Mary gratefully accepted the hot mug of coffee.

"Do you think your other roommate might know where Emma is?" asked Jenny.

"No, she dropped out a couple of weeks ago – that's why Emma and I picked up extra jobs – to make up the rent." Jenny's face flashed surprise. Emma hadn't mentioned she needed extra money to get through the semester.

Mary didn't miss the expression. "Emma didn't want to say anything to you. She said you had enough on your plate right now without having to worry about her. You know, she really, really loves you guys."

The three talked through any possible place Emma might have gone, but came up empty. Mary knew Jenny worked part-time on campus in the Theater Department, but she wasn't sure what Jenny's second job was. Emma had only had it a couple of weeks. Mary thought it was only one night a week and apparently didn't pay very much, so Emma was still looking for something more lucrative.

Caleb called the campus police, but came up empty. Although they promised they would watch for Emma, Caleb held out little hope they would find her. His cop gut instinct told him Emma had been out of touch much longer than just last night. The fact she didn't make arrangements for the kitten screamed 'warning' at him. Abandoning an animal to chance was simply something Emma could not do. He had seen her miss class, lose jobs, break-up with boyfriends - all to take care of an animal. The fact that Emma hadn't left a note for Mary meant she wasn't able to leave a note. He didn't share this insight with Jenny, but his level of concern elevated dramatically. He determined to find out just exactly when Emma had last been seen.

Though it was still the middle of the night, Caleb called the University's assistant chief of police at home. Caleb had met the University's Assistant Chief Fred Johnson at Oklahoma's CLEET Academy several years before. Fred had been Caleb's favorite guest instructor, interspersing his classes with hilarious real-life stories gleaned from his twenty years as a campus cop. The two had remained in touch since that time, seldom seeing one another, but exchanging occasional emails and professional help.

Expressing his concern as only he could do, Fred

promised to meet Caleb at the University's Police Services Building as soon as Fred could get there.

Jenny called for Jesse as she and Caleb prepared to leave. Caleb opened the front door, but Jesse had still not appeared.

Jenny went in search of the dog and found her just inside the doorway of Emma's room. The grey and white kitten was still sitting on a piece of buff paper beside the nightstand.

"Come on, Jesse," Jenny patted Jesse's back. "We've got to meet somebody." Jesse didn't move, but continued her stare at the kitten.

Behind Jenny in the hallway, Mary coughed and said, "Uh, Jenny. Look, I'll be happy to look after the kitten, but I'm gone so much of the time, and, uh, I really don't like cats....do you think you could...." Her voice trailed off.

A slight smile touched Jenny's lips. "Sure, Mary. We'll take her – or is it a him – with us." She walked across the room and bent over to pick up the kitten. Surprisingly, the kitten sunk its claws into the flyer and carried it with him into Jenny's arms. Jenny tried to extricate the paper from the kitten, but finally gave up and just brought the whole bundle along.

Caleb retrieved Emma's laptop while Mary brought the kitten's food and litter supply from the pantry in the kitchen. The whole group paraded to the front door, exchanged worried hugs and promises to call if any information came to light.

# Chapter 9

Jenny settled the two passengers in the back seat and slipped into the front beside Caleb. She usually loved coming to Edmond – especially to the east side around campus. The enormous turn-of-the century homes subdivided into student housing, the box-like apartment buildings, the smaller rental houses grossly in need of repair, and the randomly-parked, tightly-packed cars and bicycles just shouted "college town." The rustling branches of huge, overgrown trees, buckled and upturned sidewalks seemed to whisper stories of the past.

The campus itself was a beautiful mixture of the old, the new and the unusual. The oldest college building in the state was found on the far west side of the university grounds. Its architecture was "turn-of-the-century prairie" sandstone. When the University first opened its doors in 1890, this building served as the one and only classroom to train teachers in the Oklahoma territory.

Since that time, some fifty-plus buildings, library, a football stadium, baseball and soccer fields, dorms, apartments, pocket parks, and restaurants had been added. Each of the structures reflected the era in which it was built, but even though there were so many divergent styles and shapes, the campus somehow blended together harmoniously. No longer was it a "teacher's college." It was now a full-fledged university with six colleges and more than 17,000 students. Quite a change in just over one hundred and twenty years.

This night, however, Jenny dreaded her visit. Her hopes of finding a simple answer to Emma's disappearance faded with each passing block. She wanted to roll down her window and scream "Emma" into the quiet streets. But it was obvious that the sleeping community's only answer would be silence.

In the distance, Old North Tower tolled the hour slowly and deeply - almost as if it was a warning.

As the two rolled up to the campus police station, Jenny noted how plain the building was. In fact, in all her visits to the University, she had never even noticed the building at all. The unadorned rectangular brick box had apparently evaded recent campus renovations and retained its original 1940's utilitarian appearance. Or perhaps the campus administration had decided its low-key profile was just the image it wanted to convey – "No Crime Here."

**\*\*\*\*\*\*\*\*\*\***

Caleb and Jenny arrived first. The assistant chief's university car was nowhere to be seen and his parking spot was empty. After turning into a vacant place, the couple lapsed into a strained silence. There seemed to be nothing to say.

Jenny turned her attention to the kitten. "I wonder what Emma called you," she said. "I'm sure it wasn't anything usual or anything that pointed out your missing tail, either. She's much too kind for that." Jenny reached back to pick up the kitten and wound up with both the kitten and its paper in her lap.

"So why are you so attached to this?" Jenny asked as she carefully removed the flyer from the kitten's claws. In the early morning grey light, Jenny squinted to make out the words and finally discerned that the shredded flyer announced a workshop at a local non-denominational church for individuals who had lost all close family members. It was intended to help people cope with loss, survivor guilt; deal with life without close family. The workshop was scheduled to meet Thursday evenings in October and November.

"So," Jenny spoke softly into the kitten's green eyes, "have you lost someone, too?"

**\*\*\*\*\*\*\*\*\*\***

Assistant Chief Fred Johnson's bright headlights cut across Jenny's face as he wheeled into his parking spot. Quickly alighting from his SUV, Fred circled his car and came up to the driver's side as Caleb opened his door. A man of medium height and build in his mid-to late 50's, the chief had an almost handsome face and light blue eyes – eyes that had seen a lot and yet could still spark or sparkle. Just now, they were cop's eyes - concerned and wary.

The two men shook hands like old friends and Caleb introduced Jenny as she joined them. Inside the building Caleb outlined what had happened as he and Jenny removed their coats and settled in Fred's small office. Packed into every corner were photos of Fred's grandchildren. Seasoned university employees knew better than to ask about them – unless they had several hours to hear about the kids in minute detail. New campus cops were set up.

Fred started a pot of coffee, but Caleb could tell he was listening intently to each word spoken.

When Caleb paused, Fred signed on to his computer and clicked keys as Jenny gave him Emma's basic information – full name, social security number, student I.D. Almost immediately, paper spit out of the printer beside his computer. Fred handed Caleb the printout and said,

"OK, here's Emma's class schedule – along with the names of her professors – classroom locations and times of her classes. Since campus faculty and staff can't give you any information about Emma without her permission, I think it's best if I go with you to talk to her professors. That way, they'll know its okay to tell you what you need to know. These federal laws are really a pain in the ass sometimes."

\*\*\*\*\*\*\*\*\*\*

During the early morning hours, Caleb had phoned his family, the Sheriff's Office and the Clinic to let them know about Emma's disappearance. He'd been given a few days off for the family emergency and Doc Martin told Jenny to take all the time she needed.

Matt, in his typical bull-headed fashion, insisted on driving to Edmond to help. "Help – with what?" thought Caleb, but his brother would not be dissuaded.

\*\*\*\*\*\*\*\*\*\*

It was well past 10:00 that Saturday morning when Jenny and Caleb connected with the first of Emma's professors.

They found Dr. Amanda Sloan, Emma's major advisor, in Mitchell Hall, the University's 1930's vintage theater. Although the theater had recently undergone renovation with new lighting, seating, and a state-of-the-art sound system, the architects had gone to great lengths to retain the beauty and charm of its original construction.

Jenny and Caleb felt they were stepping into a bygone era when they entered the theater's art deco lobby. Old black and white prints highlighting past University productions lined the walls. Red velvet corded stanchions assured audiences entered the productions in good order.

The two made their way into the heart of the theater carefully, as their eyes had not yet adjusted to the gloom of the unlit house seats. They sat front row, center to wait.

On stage a short, plump raven-haired woman skillfully directed a frenzied chaos of student writers, directors, actors, prop managers and costumers. Jenny couldn't understand how anyone could function in all the frenetic activity, but apparently these people thrived on it.

In truth, Dr. Sloan did not even have to be on campus on Saturday – unless, of course, there was a performance. Then wild horses couldn't keep her away. But with the upcoming one-act play performances as the semester's primary project, she was making herself available for her anxious, over-stressed student advisees.

Just as Caleb and Jenny sat down to wait for Dr. Sloan, Matt strode into the theater. He spotted them immediately, hurried forward and plopped down next to his brother.

Caleb brought him up to speed with what little

information he and Jenny had been able to gather, but Matt wanted more than just information. He was inconsolable and bristling to act.

As much as just giving him something to do as anything else, Jenny asked Matt to check out the church grief counseling flyer she'd found in Emma's room.

Caleb asked Jenny if she had any recent photos of Emma. Jenny searched her purse, but could come up with only one – Emma's high school graduation picture. Emma's hair was much longer then and it was several shades darker, but it was the best Jenny could do.

"Matt, take the photo to the copy shop down on 2nd Street and have some copies made before you go to the church, OK? They may come in handy."

Matt grabbed the shredded paper flyer and the photo from Jenny and headed out the west doors almost at a run.

**\*\*\*\*\*\*\*\*\***

When Dr. Sloan had tended to the most critical of her students' needs, she gracefully descended the steps stage right and made her way to the seating out front, where the Tallchiefs anxiously waited.

"You're Emma's sister and brother-in-law, aren't you? Fred – Chief Johnson - called and said you'd be by. I can't tell you how sorry I am about Emma. I should have known something was wrong when she didn't keep her 8:30 appointment yesterday. Her one-act play was really important to her and she was working so hard to keep it real…..she is so very talented, you know." Dr. Sloan's hand fluttered with every word, whether for emphasis or just a part of her dramatic flair, Jenny wasn't sure.

Although Caleb thought he recognized the former professional actress from some of the classic movies he and Jenny loved watching, he didn't mention it. Instead, he went straight to the heart of the matter.

"Is there anything you can tell us that might help us find Emma?"

Jenny didn't even wait for the professor to answer, but rapid-fired her questions. "Can you think of anywhere Emma might have gone? Do you know if she has a steady boyfriend here? Or have you seen her with anyone new lately?" Caleb took Jenny's hand.

Dr. Sloan, somewhat flustered with questions battering her in stereo, finally responded. "Well, let me think…..I believe she did have someone she was seeing – but that was last spring semester and I think he graduated or something. He wasn't a theater major, you know, so I don't know much about him."

She continued, "Emma did mention something about a new man in her life the last time I reviewed her play. Let's see – it was Matt or Mike or …. I'm sorry, I just don't remember other than it started with an 'M' sound – at least I think it was an 'M' sound – could have been an 'N.' Not much help, I know." Her hands fluttered.

"Is there anything at all you can remember that might help?" Caleb urged again. "Any little detail might give us a clue as to where she might be or what she might have been thinking about."

Dr. Sloan pondered the question. "The last time we talked, I told Emma her play was coming along really well, but that she had to beef up the persona of the leading character."

"You see, the play was about a young woman who had just lost her entire family in a freak accident and the emotional state of the young woman was critical in the play's development. Although the story was already very good, I knew with a little extra "umph," it could be an exceptional one. I suggested she visit with our Psychology Department about the ways in which grief manifests itself and she said she would."

"I just can't think of anything else we discussed. I know this hasn't been much help....maybe she's just decided everything is too much for her right now and she's gone off by herself." Dr. Sloan looked up hopefully at the pair and waived her hands around some more. "I guess that's not very realistic, is it?"

"No," said Jenny. "Emma would never disappear voluntarily."

Caleb rose, handing the teacher contact information. "Thank you, Dr. Sloan. If you think of anything else –

anything else at all, please call Jenny or me – day or night."

Dr. Sloan stood up and took Jenny's hand in hers. Her stage persona slipped away and she said, "I hope you find her very soon. Emma is a very special person. She has a rare talent, but more than that, she is a lovely human being."

Tears welled in her eyes as she turned away and returned to the melee on the stage.

**********

Caleb and Jenny emerged from the box office and lobby area of Mitchell Hall into the bright November sunshine. The preceding spring and summer had blessed the area with more rain than most years and the remaining leaves on the trees still echoed the vibrant colors of fall. The many plaques and engraved bricks making up the walkways spoke to the many years the theater had entertained and educated artists and audiences.

Jenny noticed none of it. Her eyes were downcast and her heart was in her throat. "Where can we go from here?" she asked forlornly.

"How about if we call Fred Johnson and see where he is in arranging meetings with Emma's other professors? Maybe we can talk to the psychology folks. Dr. Sloan sent her there for help with her play; maybe we can get a lead."

As the two began walking across the campus to the Police Services Building, Caleb's phone bagpiped its familiar "Scotland the Brave." Caleb answered and, almost as if it was scripted, Fred Johnson's voice blasted in his ear.

"Hey, Cal. I've gotten ahold of Dr. Ray Knight, the department chair for Psychology. Well, truthfully Dr. Sloan called him and told him what's going on. He's agreed to meet us in his office as soon as we can get there. Meet me outside Police Services and we'll walk over together."

"Thanks, Fred. We're on our way."

\*\*\*\*\*\*\*\*\*\*

Dr. Ray Knight was a tall, athletic-looking man in his mid-fifties. His hair was entirely gray and he sported a short-cropped beard of gray and black. "The only thing missing is the pipe," thought Caleb as he and Jenny sat either side of Fred Johnson.

"Dr. Sloan called me about Emma," he said, "and I'm really concerned. She just started working for the department last month on a special project – actually it's a joint project between our department and the University Counseling Center. She's compiling a list of resources in and around the Edmond area for our students to access or for possible internship positions."

"I just reviewed her initial research last Monday. She said she only had a few more places to check out." He opened a side drawer of his old, battered desk, fumbled around inside for a minute, pulled out a pipe, and began to fill it.

Fred asked, "Can you give us a list of the places she visited – and anyone she might have contacted at each of them? Maybe that will help us narrow down her movements."

Dr. Knight set his pipe aside, mumbling, "Can't smoke the damn thing here anyway," and walked over to a work table in the corner. Finally, after some shuffling of papers and rearranging a stack of books, he straightened up with a sheaf of papers.

"Here's a copy of her initial research – let me copy it for you." He headed out the door and the trio could soon hear him cursing the machine. Finally, the hum of copying filled the hallway and Dr. Knight reappeared with a second set of papers.

"Emma came in about a month ago, looking for a second campus job. She was highly recommended by Amanda Sloan – and believe me, those recommendations are few and far between. So I hired her for this special project."

Jenny quickly scanned the list and noted one of the places was the one on the flyer in Emma's room. The group discussed this and other possibilities for the next couple of minutes, but didn't come up with any revelations.

Fred, Jenny and Caleb left to discuss what their next step should be.

# Chapter 10

Just thirty-five hours earlier, Emma Cochran had attended the fourth session of the "Grief Seminar," sponsored by the Life Today Non-Denominational Church.

She felt a little twinge of guilt as she looked around the circle of grief-stricken participants. There were some her age, some older, one younger, but all were living through the trauma of significant loss. Emma felt just a little bit dishonest posing as someone without any family at all. It was true she had lost her parents, but, it had happened so long ago, she seldom felt the loss anymore.

She'd just stopped by Life Today Church last month to find out what types of classes and seminars they routinely offered to add to her research list for the Psychology Department. As she was picking up brochures, the flyer announcing the grief seminar caught her eye.

At first, it seemed almost providential. Here was the perfect place to get some 'realism' into her play. Her mind raced. She could attend the seminar as someone who had lost her family – in the persona of her lead character, Jenna Ryan, in fact. Yes, she could learn a lot at this workshop. Spur-of-the-moment, she signed herself up as "Jenna" for the seminar. Only her first name and a brief summary of her family situation were required to participate. It was easy.

Now Emma was rethinking her snap decision. Unfortunately, there was no way she could tell the truth now. Too much raw emotion had been shared during these sessions for her to reveal her losses were actually only part of her one-act play. Better she just stop going. Emma decided this would be her last class.

"Thank God," Emma thought. "I'm not like the rest of these poor people – all alone in this world. I have Jenny and Caleb." Jenny had been Emma's sister, her mom, and her best friend for as long as Emma could remember. And Caleb – well, he was the perfect brother. Although lately - well, lately she'd been thinking a lot about allowing Matt into her exclusive family circle, too.

Thinking of Matt made Emma smile.

"Thinking of your family?" John asked as he sat down next to Emma.

Emma jerked back to reality. "No, not really. How are you, John?"

"I think better this week…especially since you're

here, Jenna. I don't know what I'd do if I couldn't see you every week."

Emma shuttered internally. She really didn't want John's attention. Then she immediately chastised herself for such selfish thoughts. She forced herself to smile at the young man. After all, John had recently lost his mother to cancer. And his mother had been his only family. The poor man was now alone in the world. This was her last session; she could afford to be kind.

Emma felt John's pain when he talked about his mother last week. She really did feel sorry for him – but the way in which he had attached himself to her made her very uncomfortable. He was nice to look at – but there was just something a bit off about him. She really couldn't put her finger on what it was, but – his presence made the hair on the back of her neck stand up. John and his mother had been very close, and John had nursed her through years of illness. That in itself would make someone weird. But she didn't want to make John even weirder by disappearing from the program without some kind of explanation.

"You know, John, people sometimes get attached for the wrong reasons. When they're emotionally vulnerable, they can think there's more going on in a relationship than there really is …. I've been thinking that myself. Maybe this isn't the right kind of a program for me. This may be my last time…." Emma stumbled into silence. Luckily, one of the other participants came in and sat on the other side of Emma. Emma turned from John as she and the new arrival exchanged hellos.

John stared at Emma for a long time before shifting his gaze to his hands.

**********

John Tyler had been watching Jenna Ryan/Emma Cochran for more than three weeks. He knew that, this time, he had made the correct choice. She was beautiful, funny, and loving. He watched as she interacted with the others in the group – always supportive and kind, even though she had been through such a trauma in her own life.

She looked so much like his own mother with her petite stature, curly blonde hair and laughing eyes. Yes, she was absolutely perfect. She was smart, too. Not like those domestic cows his brothers had married. When they saw her they'd be green with envy – he would have the most perfect, loving wife. None of them would ever doubt what a man he was when he had such a perfect woman at his side. Kids, too, lots of them - and that would shut the old man up.

John Tyler's life had not been an easy one. His father was a brutal man – a trait carried on in both of his older sons. Even though John was his mother's favorite and she tried her best to protect him, John suffered interminable and often cruel hazing from his brothers.

His father would only step in when John was in danger of becoming seriously injured. John could never muster the courage it took to stand up to them. His brothers thought him a coward. Worse, his father thought him effeminate.

It hadn't been quite so bad when John was very young. He and his brothers would accompany their father into the deep woods and hunt. John loved the darkness and silence he found there and learned he had a natural talent for tracking and killing wildlife.

John could almost predict where the next doe or buck would be found. When his father brought down a deer, John was fascinated. He most enjoyed the moment of the kill, when his father would put the final shot into a wounded deer or coyote. John's father would even boast of his youngest's ability to "man up" when the going got tough.

It was later that John's problems really began. Even though he was attractive, medium height, great build, sandy brown hair, blue eyes, an impish boy countenance, he had always had a difficult time with girls. John always treated them well – too well in the opinion of his macho brothers. Girls just didn't want to be around him. After one or two dates, none of them wished to go out with him again. John didn't understand it. His father and his brothers teased him relentlessly about it. They told him he'd never get laid.

Then there was that one regrettable incident in his senior year of high school with another boy that had branded them both "homos." From his family's perspective, this was the unforgiveable sin. His father beat him bloody, broke his right arm, and would have no more to do with him. Even his mother was ashamed. John became a pariah and the butt of all the cruel jokes his brothers could invent.

After his mother died, John became even more estranged from his remaining family. He suffered through the rest of his senior year, but following graduation, he determined he had to get away from his lethal home environment.

John volunteered to set up a collegiate network to sell a portion of the family's marijuana crop both in Oklahoma and northeast Texas. For John, this was the best of all worlds. He could evade his brothers' cruelty and his father's indifference and return to his beloved woods.

It was a win-win for John's family, too. They were thrilled to have their embarrassment of a brother and son out of sight and mind. John selected one of the backwoods cabins owned by his family as his home base and never looked back.

The move turned out to be a stroke of genius. John was an outstanding organizer and astute businessman. His enterprise became wildly successful, even earning him some grudging respect from his father.

John loved the power his new position brought him. He was no longer the punching bag for his older brothers. He was in charge – in command and determined to stay that way. His past acquiescent personality was no more. His subordinates jumped when he spoke or soon regretted their lapse.

Another advantage of John's new business was the opportunity to shop for the perfect wife. He hadn't considered this aspect when he first proposed setting up his network, but the idea came to him as he established his college contact distributors.

John thought he'd found just the right woman several times over the last few years, but he'd been wrong. None of them had been right. But now everything had worked out for the best, because he was certain that Jenna was the one he'd been searching for all along. She was perfect.

However, her revelation that she was thinking about leaving the seminar threw John into a panic. He wasn't quite prepared to propose yet, but then again, he was always prepared. He knew one of the hallmarks of success in business was to be ready to move quickly when the situation called for immediate action.

He would take Jenna tonight.

**********

At the end of the session, John asked if he could walk Emma to her car. Or maybe they could go out for coffee.

"No, but thanks, John. I've got to study tonight. I'm

going to get some hot chocolate to drink on the way home. It's pretty cold out there and the heater in my car doesn't work worth a flip."

"Yeah, that sounds pretty good. I think I'll get some, too." John followed Emma to the drink table and waited as she filled up a cup and turned away.

"Here, Jenna. Let me put a lid on that for you. You don't want to spill that all over you or your car on the way home." Without giving Emma a chance to decline, John took Emma's cup from her hand and turned away to put a travel lid on it. Unknown to Emma, he also slipped some GHB into her chocolate before returning the cup to her. He was very smooth. She never suspected a thing. He only gave her a small amount. He didn't want a repeat of that fiasco in Sherman, Texas, when that girl up and died. You just never knew what those crazy drug cookers put in this stuff.

"Is it too hot?" John asked.

Emma took a small sip and made a face. "No, no - it's fine. Thanks, John. See you."

Truthfully, the chocolate was awful. It tasted bitter and salty. But Emma was anxious to get away from John. She wanted to get to her car before John could pour his drink and follow her. She quick-stepped toward the front door.

By the time Emma reached her car, her stomach was roiling. "I guess I shouldn't have skipped dinner," she thought as she fumbled for her keys, unlocked the door and almost fell into the driver's seat. The sense of nausea grew and, suddenly John appeared, knocking at her window. She rolled it down partway.

"Are you okay?" he asked, his face anxious with worry.

"Yesh, um, well, no….I'm not feeling….. good…." Although Emma tried to focus, her vision blurred and she was very dizzy. She didn't seem able to speak coherently.

John continued to lean into the car, appearing to talk to Emma, although she was no longer capable of responding. She'd passed out cold.

He waited until the parking lot had cleared, even waving to a few of the late departing seminar attendees. If asked, they'd just say they'd seen him talking to Emma after the session had ended. He was safe. No one knew his last name and he'd never be back here again. When he was sure everyone was gone, John gently lifted Emma from her driver's seat and placed her into the passenger side of his pickup.

No one was there to see his taillights disappear into the chilly, black November night.

# Chapter 11

Matt Tallchief threw open the double door at the main entrance to Life Today Church, a mega non-denominational religious institution. It had an enormous television following and offered a multitude of community services. His footfall echoed as he marched along, unsure as to which of the several halls leading off the main lobby he should take.

An attractive college-age woman passed him on his left, and, recognizing his indecision, said, "Hi. I'm Casey. Can I help you find something?"

"Thanks," Matt extended his hand. "I'm Matt Tallchief. I guess I'm looking for someone who can tell me about this," Matt answered, holding out the tattered flyer.

"Oh, yeah. That's one of the new sessions our Program Director is trying out this fall. I haven't been to it myself, but I believe it's been pretty well attended. Let me take you to Dr. Adams. He should be able to help you."

After winding their way through a maze of corridors and smaller lobbies, they stopped at a door marked "Marvin Adams, D.D./Program Director."

Casey stuck her head in the open doorway and was motioned in. She introduced Matt to the young minister behind the functional pseudo wood computer desk. Then she raised her hand in a brief good-bye, backed out of the room, and closed the door behind her.

Dr. Adams peered at Matt through his round eye glasses, stood and shook his hand. "How can I help you? It's Matt, right?"

"Right. Thanks, I hardly know where to start. My sister-in-law's sister, Emma Cochran, has disappeared and we're pretty worried. She was supposed to come home to Tecumseh yesterday and never showed up. We're trying to find her."

Matt put the flyer on the desk, facing the minister. "One of the things we found in her room was this flyer, and I was wondering if you could tell me anything about it."

Dr. Adams picked up the flyer. "Yes, yes, this is ours. This is the first time we're offering this type of seminar and so far it's going really well. It's amazing how many people in and around our area have suffered such significant losses. We just don't have any idea of how hard it is to be so alone as most of us have lots of family and friends. But these people do not. They have no one."

He thought for a moment, "We don't have a young

woman in our program named Emma," he said. Matt handed him Emma's high school photo.

"Well, she looks a little like a woman in the program named Jenna, but it really can't be her. Jenna doesn't have any family. I believe they were all killed in a house fire last spring while she was away at college. She doesn't have anyone."

Adams continued, "You see, that's the common link among all the people who are attending this seminar. They're all people without families. So, it can't be the same person."

Noting Matt's disappointment, he added, "You know, we distribute those flyers all around town and even on the college campus. She may have just picked it up."

He paused, his eyes now reflecting a somewhat disinterested sympathy. "I don't think I can really help you." His voice took on a tone of dismissal as he returned the flyer to Matt.

Disheartened, Matt returned to his pickup, walking slowly and thinking. As he pulled open the door, he glanced around the almost-deserted parking lot and a smear of faded red caught his eye.

Matt ran hell-bent-for-leather toward the vehicle to find Emma's clunky, seldom running, rusted red Ford. The car was unlocked and her purse and a spilled coffee cup were in the passenger floor board. Emma was no where to be seen.

# Chapter 12

The '96 Chevy pickup hit a pothole and jarred Emma into a semi-conscious state. "What's...." she began to speak, but her voice cracked and ceased to make any noise.

"Don't worry, sweetheart. You'll feel better pretty soon. Here, drink some water," John fumbled in the cooler behind her seat and handed her a plastic water bottle. Emma couldn't make her hands open the screw top and John smiled. With an almost parental sigh, John pulled over to the side of the road and uncapped the bottle for Emma, held it to her lips and allowed her to drink. "Now, Jenna. Just a little bit. We don't want you to be sick again, do we?"

Emma didn't remember being sick. As a matter of fact, she didn't remember much of anything at all. She barely registered that her ankles were bound by a chain and attached to an eyebolt screwed into the floorboard.

"Oh well. It doesn't really matter," she thought, as she slumped over and drifted back into sleep.

**\*\*\*\*\*\*\*\*\*\***

Matt paced back and forth behind Emma's little red Ford. He knew better than to touch anything before his brother got there, but it seemed like he had been waiting an eternity before he saw the familiar SUV turn into the parking lot.

Caleb alighted from his side of the car and Jenny burst from the passenger side. Jesse, too, seemed anxious to help. She smelled all four tires almost as an affirmation that the car did, indeed, belong to their missing Emma. She also had the good sense not to mark any of them.

Caleb verified it was Emma's car and noted her purse and car keys still in the front seat. He called Fred Johnson to let him know they had found Emma's car. Then he called the Edmond police department and requested assistance.

It was just a few minutes before two City of Edmond police cars wheeled into the parking lot, followed closely by Chief Bauman's black and white SUV. His good friend and colleague, Fred Johnson, had alerted him to Emma's disappearance, and the chief wanted to see this new development for himself.

Caleb, Matt and Jenny shared what information

they had learned from Emma's professors with Chief Mike Bauman. Even though the chief knew a missing person's report was generally not filed until a person had been gone for more than 48 hours, he recognized that Caleb, as a professional law enforcement officer, would be more clear-headed than most in his analysis of the situation. That, and the fact, Emma's purse and keys remained in the Ford, led him to move forward quickly. Sometimes 48 hours was too long to wait – and something told him that might be the case now.

"Caleb, I want you and Jenny to fill out a missing persons report right now," he said. "You can follow me to the station. In the meantime," he gestured to the patrolmen, "you two secure the site and wait for the forensics team to get here."

Since they knew practically nothing, it didn't take too long to complete the report. After the paperwork was done, the chief told them to go home and get some rest. He promised to keep them informed of any development as soon as it happened.

Having effectively been dismissed from what was now an official Edmond police investigation, the trio returned to Tecumseh. Even though they had no official standing, they were still determined to do whatever they could to find Emma.

# Chapter 13

Emma slowly came back to consciousness in the early morning hours of Friday. The sun had not yet appeared, but the black night had begun its slow transition into gray.

"John, where are we? What's going on?"

John turned his eyes from the road to meet Emma's worried ones. "Jenna, don't you worry about a thing. Everything will be just perfect. I knew from the minute I saw you that you and I were meant to be together. We're both alone in this world and now we have each other – just the two of us."

"I don't understand. Where are we?" Emma moved and her leg pulled tight against the chain around her ankle. "What is this?" she screamed. "Do you have me tied up?"

"Look I said, don't worry." John's gentle manner vanished. "I'm going to take good care of you. We're going to be together and love each other and take care of each other, understand?"

The instant shift in John's personality set off loud warning bells in Emma's mind.

"I don't….."

"Don't what?" He spat out the words and his eyes bored into hers – almost as a challenge to disagree.

She looked at his wild eyes. "Nothing"

"Good."

\*\*\*\*\*\*\*\*\*\*

Since John had not intended to take Emma that evening, he had to do some quick mental and physical rescheduling. He was able to cancel a couple of his stops, but others could not be postponed.

He had to meet two of his distributors and make some deliveries. People expected their product on time – even a day or two made a difference. It had taken him too long to build his network and didn't want anything to jeopardize that.

Tyler reasoned this would not really be a problem, since he had enough GHB to keep Jenna drugged. Since he was not sure how the multiple doses of GHB would affect her, he'd keep them very small and make sure she got plenty of water and some food, too. He really didn't want to put his "fiancé" at risk – but she'd understand.

After all, he was doing all of this for both of them – wasn't he?

**********

It was late evening before John and Emma neared Harley. John watched as his gas gauge slowly dipped toward the red zone. He figured he had enough gas to get to the cabin, but didn't want to take the chance.

There was a small convenience store just a few miles down the road where he could fill up and buy a few supplies. Stopping there should be no problem. Emma was still groggy, slipping in and out of sleep – but giving him no problems. No doubt, she'd be out until they got to the cabin.

In reality, Emma was much more alert than she appeared. She had a splitting headache, but she recognized she was in real trouble. With her eyes shut and feinting sleep, she tried to figure out a way to escape from this madman. She tossed and turned, testing the limits of her constraints, but so far, she had been unable to detect any way to get free.

John veered over onto the shoulder just before reaching the turn-off into the store's parking lot.

"Jenna, wake up." He shook her gently. "I need you to listen to me." John firmly cupped Emma's chin with his right hand and turned it toward him. "Can you hear me?"

Emma nodded and slightly opened her eyes.

"We've got to get some gas and some food at a little store up ahead. I don't want you to talk to anybody, understand? Nobody. If you do, I'll have to punish you, you understand? I'll have to punish anybody you talk to, too. You don't want that, do you?"

Emma's eyes opened further. She certainly didn't want herself or anyone else hurt.

**\*\*\*\*\*\*\*\*\*\***

John scanned the parking lot of the Turney's Country Store before pulling in. "Lucky," he thought, "it's empty and just about dark, too. Nobody will be able to see inside the truck."

Tyler pulled the pickup alongside the gas pump, got out and walked back to the unleaded. He flipped up the on/off switch, but the gas pump would not turn on. He tried it several times before throwing up his hands in frustration and striding into the store.

Emma rolled down her window in the hopes the cool air would further clear her mind. As she gazed across the parking lot, she heard a metallic noise rattle just behind and to her left. As she turned to look, a boy suddenly appeared at her side. Emma was terrified for him and hoped the body of the pickup would shield him from view in the grocery store.

The young teenager – he appeared to be about

thirteen – pulled at the brim of his hat and said, "I fixed the lever on the gas pump. It sticks sometimes. You should be able to pump gas now. Do you want me to start it for you?

"No," Emma blurted out quickly. "No, we'll do it. Thank you, anyway." She willed the boy to get away from the truck.

With some difficulty, the boy corralled and then picked up the large dog that had been furiously sniffing the pickup truck's bed. The animal had a lackluster and somewhat spotty fur coat and was so thin his ribs showed. But his tail wagged rapid-fire as he licked his owner's face and wiggled in his arms. The boy rocked back and forth on his heels trying to balance the big chocolate-colored animal.

Emma quickly glanced around again while she just as quickly considered her options. She knew this might be her only chance to pass along a message, but it had to be something John would never know was a cry for help; something that would not put the boy at risk.

"Um, your dog looks kind of sick."

"Yeah, we don't know what's wrong with him – even the vet can't figure it out. He won't eat and he's so tired I have to carry him around sometimes. His name's Zeppy – after some ancient band my Granna really loved."

"You know, there's this wonderful vet in Tecumseh named Dr. Tallchief. They've got this medicine called the honey cure that I'm sure would really help what ails

Zeppy. But you really need to call right away – today, OK? Talk only to Dr. Tallchief..." she spoke hurriedly. "Can you remember that name?

"Sure," said the young teen. "Dr. Tallchief, Tecumseh, honey cure. Thanks, lady."

John burst through the front door of the Turney's Country Store, his arms full of grocery bags. He spied the boy beside Emma. "Hey, kid. Get the hell away from there," he screamed.

The young man quickly backed away from the pickup. John threw the grocery bags in the bed of the truck, whirled and grabbed the young teen by the front of his jacket.

Tyler pulled the kid's face up to his and demanded, "What did she say to you?"

Zeppy, unceremoniously dropped on the ground at the teen's feet, barked furiously as he tried to stand.

"Nothin', mister. She just told me to call a vet about my sick dog – that's all."

"You sure that's all she said – everything?"

The child was terrified, "Yeah, honest. That's it."

John threw the young man down on the ground and jumped into the pickup.

He turned to Emma. "I told you not to talk to anyone. I warned you."

Emma looked pleadingly at John and took his hand. She intoned in a soft voice, "Look, John. His poor dog is sick. You wouldn't want it to suffer needlessly, would you?"

She kept her eyes on his. "You're a good man – you know what it's like to lose someone you love. That's all it was. I'm sorry. I'm very sorry. OK?"

Emma put all the charm and sympathy into her voice and expression she could muster – almost as if her life depended on convincing him there was no harm done. A small voice inside her said it just might.

John thought a moment, breathed deeply, and slowly brought his temper under control. Damn it - nothing was going according to plan this time.

Finally, "You know, my mom loved dogs, too. OK, OK. No harm done, I guess. You've had your one mistake. Next time…" Emma didn't even want to think about what would happen next time.

Tyler didn't wait to fill up the tank. He just turned on the engine, shoved the transmission into drive and threw gravel as they regained the highway.

# Chapter 14

Immediately upon their return to Tecumseh Saturday night, Jenny, Caleb, and Matt met around the kitchen table to brainstorm their next step. None of them could wait for the Edmond Police. They had to do something – even if it got them nowhere.

Caleb's family gathered around, bringing food and support to the conclave. Possibilities for action whirled around the table – some realistic and most not.

Sometime during the evening, Jenny noticed an unfamiliar face among the crowd. Caleb's grandfather, Joe Tallchief, drew Jenny aside and introduced her to Paul White Horse, a full-blood Seminole.

At first glance, the man appeared as old and withered as the ancient acacia tree outside their front door. He was dressed unremarkably in jeans, work boots, a tan wool-lined jacket and a beat-to-hell straw cowboy hat. His stout body was weathered and deeply tanned - even though it was November. The man's face was furrowed and wrinkled with deep laugh lines.

But it was his aura that most captivated Jenny. She could not describe it – the man was a presence that was somehow "more" than any other person she had ever met.

The old man took Jenny's hands in his and gazed into her eyes with a rheumy, brown stare – full of understanding and sorrow. Jenny, normally skittish about being touched, felt somehow secure with this man – somehow safe and at peace.

White Horse suggested he and Jenny take a walk outside in the crisp November air and Jenny agreed. Jesse trotted silently at her side.

The night was cold and clear and the stars twinkled silently above. But Jenny did not feel the temperature nor did she notice the brightness of the stars. Her thoughts were dark and troubled.

Jesse trotted beside the two, perfectly content in the presence of the tall stranger.

Paul White Horse talked almost poetically about the beauty of the night – of the land – and of the history of his people. Instead of feeling she was being taken away from the really important work going on around her kitchen table, Jenny listened intently. Even Jesse seemed to be interested in what the old man had to say.

They strolled on – the only sounds the crunching of

their footsteps on the frosty dirt and their chilled breath as it met the night air.

"You know, Jenny," White Horse began. "You have been given a great gift."

Jenny looked at him quizzically.

"You are able to see into the heart of many of God's creatures and know things others cannot."

Jenny nodded slowly; understanding that he was somehow aware of her unusual connection to the animals she touched.

"I, too," he continued, "can see into the minds and souls of animals. Although I think not as well as you."

Jenny paused a moment and, with a sigh, decided she would trust this man. "This touching – this sensing – it scares me. I don't know what to do – whether it's real or it's something I'm just making up. Sometimes I think I'm going insane." She rambled.

White Horse seemed to have no trouble tracking her train of thought. "Maybe you are just moving into a new level of sanity," he said.

Then he chuckled, "I guess acknowledging such a thing is possible is easier for me," he said. "My culture and training taught me that all life is part of us. That we are all interconnected."

"So," he continued, "you're probably wondering why I have come – why we're having this conversation?

Jenny nodded.

"I asked Joe to introduce us. He and I have been close friends since childhood – even though we're not of the same tribe. Not everyone is lucky enough to be Seminole, you know." He chuckled again.

Sensing Jenny was in no mood for humor, he continued solemnly, "I have a message and a warning for you. I want you to know you are not losing your mind. There are many of us who know there is a much greater range of intelligent life on this planet and in this universe than humankind ever envisioned. You are just coming to know that. You must trust what you feel. You must follow your instincts and what is shared by others, even if that information comes from a – let's say - an unconventional source."

"In fact, it is my personal belief that most animals – other than human beings - are much more worthy of our trust – they don't know how to lie or deceive." He smiled at his own wisdom.

Jenny stared at him, part of her accepting his words and part of her questioning his hold on reality.

White Horse spoke, "My friends tell me there is a great evil holding your sister and that you must find her quickly. I don't know where she is, but I do know she is in great danger."

"The evil holding her captive has killed many times before and will continue to kill until he is stopped. He kills not out of necessity but for the sheer joy of killing. You and Caleb must hurry."

They walked on in silence for a few more steps.

"I have a gift for you – something I made with much prayer and meditation." White Horse pressed a short braided leather cord, strung through a small beaded circle into her hand.

"When you begin to question yourself, take this talisman into your hands and press it against your heart. It will speak the truth to you." His message conveyed, White Horse nodded once for emphasis, then turned and walked quietly into the darkness.

Jenny didn't know what to say. She didn't know what to think. She knew running after this man would yield her no more information, but she didn't see how any of this would help her find Emma.

Jenny returned to the light and chaos of her kitchen feeling no wiser and more confused than ever. Her father-in-law glanced up and gave Jenny a knowing nod – as if Paul White Horse's message had solved everything.

\*\*\*\*\*\*\*\*\*\*

During her absence, Caleb, Matt and the rest of the Tallchief family had come up with a predictable, if uninspired, plan of action. Caleb had decided to put what information he had out on the Sheriff's Association list serve. Joe had suggested looking into other missing person reports to see if there might be any similarities. Anna, Caleb's mother, thought they should check out the grief seminar angle.

Matt just looked forlorn and pissed off at the same time.

\*\*\*\*\*\*\*\*\*\*

Caleb drove the ten miles from his house to the Sheriff's Office in Shawnee to post his inquiry on the Sheriff's list serve and to see if any new information from the Edmond police had come in. He also wanted to pull any missing person reports he had access to and see if anything could be learned from them.

\*\*\*\*\*\*\*\*\*\*

Back at the Tallchief kitchen table, Anna and Matt tackled the grief seminar angle. Matt called Dr. Adams at Life Today Church to see if he could get a list of other venues in which the seminar had been held.

Dr. Adams, still full of angst over the probable abduction of a young woman from his church's parking lot, readily agreed to do whatever he could to help. He said he'd do some calling around and put together the list as soon as he could.

By midnight, Caleb had returned. He'd posted the request for information on the list serve, and had also requested copies of persons who had been reported missing anywhere in the state during the last five years. Now all they could do was wait.

**\*\*\*\*\*\*\*\*\*\***

First thing Sunday morning Caleb called Chief Bauman requesting an update. He was told the liquid in the coffee cup had been sent to the OSBI lab for analysis. Emma's car had been fingerprinted and, as with the liquid analysis, the prints were being run against all pertinent databases.

The other contents of the vehicle were also under scrutiny, but so far, nothing appeared to be out of the ordinary – a plethora of fast food wrappers, papers, receipts, books, a hoodie – Emma was not the most tidy of persons – gave the Edmond forensics unit a lot of items to sift through.

The chief promised he would let Caleb know the minute he had any information.

Jenny and Caleb drove into the Sheriff's Office and nodded to the officer manning the phones.

"Sheriff's in the back. Said to send you back there soon as you got here."

Caleb went through the door, mentally formulating what he could say to the Chief, because, the truth of the matter was - he'd used county resources on a case that was personal – the investigation into Emma's disappearance belonged to the Edmond Police Department.

They found Sheriff Holcomb sifting through the missing person reports that had come in overnight as a result of Caleb's request.

"Cal, you know this is something we're supposed to leave to Edmond. Not in our jurisdiction…

Caleb started to respond, but Holcomb held up his hand and brusquely cut him off. He motioned for Caleb and Jenny to sit. "So, how about we get started?"

The Sheriff pulled a chair out for Jenny and handed her a stack of reports. Relief flooded through Caleb.

Holcomb continued, "I just checked the list serve site, and a couple counties have already responded. Nothing I could see was of any use, but you can look if you've a mind to." Caleb shook his head. If the Sheriff said there was nothing in the responses – then there was nothing.

They turned to see Mary Ellen Moore's ample figure fill the doorway. She carried a box overflowing with sandwiches, chips and some soft drinks.

"Figured we'd need something to eat. Now, anybody want coffee? "

********** 

First, each of them read through all the missing person reports. From time to time, one of them would check to see if anything new trickled in. Then they discussed how to prioritize. With more than 100 missing person cases in hand, there was no way they had the manpower to reinvestigate them all.

After some back and forth debate, they finally settled on dividing the reports into categories with young women – women in their late teens to mid-twenties - as the highest priority. By the time they finished categorizing all one hundred plus cases, it was early afternoon. In all, fifteen made it to the final cut.

Mary Ellen had to go home, but Caleb, Jenny, and Sheriff Holcomb carefully scrutinized the fifteen once more, hoping they'd missed something. They had. In nine of the reports, the missing person had disappeared while attending college, and in three of the cases; the report had been filed by a boyfriend, a roommate or a professor. "That's weird," noted Jenny. "Why didn't their families report them missing?"

Sheriff Holcomb volunteered to contact the sheriff in the counties and/or the chief of police in the towns from which the nine females had gone missing to see if there had been any further developments. One of the women had been missing for more than three years, so perhaps some clue had come to light since the initial report that would help them track Emma.

Caleb and Jenny left the Sheriff to his task and returned home to check on developments there.

# Chapter 15

After they left the grocery store, John forced Emma to drink some more "doctored" water. He needed some time to think and plan the next few days without interference.

Emma fell asleep and stayed asleep for most of Saturday and Sunday. John was able to get her to drink a little, but she fought him when he tried to get her to eat and collapsed back into sleep. So instead of thinking or planning, Tyler spent the next 48 hours sitting by Emma's side, alternately disparaging himself for giving her so much of the drug and cursing the crazy Mexican bastard who cooked it.

John was closely monitoring Emma when she finally awoke in the predawn darkness early Monday morning. Luckily, her head was relatively clear. John breathed a sigh of relief – who would have guessed it would take that long to flush the drugs from her system?

When Emma opened her eyes and gazed about,

she found herself lying on a double bed, covered with a heavy down comforter and hand-made quilt. The bed was in a room that looked to be about 17 x 20 feet.

She could see a small galley kitchen lit by under-the-counter lights, a large stone fireplace and a doorway that probably led to a bathroom. The room appeared to be well-furnished with a small kitchen table and two chairs, a recliner, a large hand made chest and the single bed in which she lay. She didn't notice the small antique roll top desk tucked into the far corner. A roaring fire played in the stacked stone fireplace.

At first, Emma was confused – uncertain as to why she was in this room or what had happened. But when she turned to relieve the soreness in her back, she looked right into the eyes of her captor. Flashes of memory from the last few days came rushing back. Emma tried to get up from the bed only to find she was tethered by her ankle to a long chain attached to the fireplace.

When she looked pitifully at John, he explained, "That's only for now, sweetheart. Just as soon as we get to know each other better – I'll take the chain off."

He smiled paternally, "For now, you can move all around the cabin, use the bathroom, get something to eat – anything but go outside. But you wouldn't want to do that anyway. It's colder than hell out there. Now let me get you something to eat."

Emma didn't know how to react. She obviously was the prisoner of someone both insane and dangerous. She needed time to think – to plan. Plus, she really had to use the bathroom.

"John, I need to use the bathroom. I need to take a shower."

"Sure, Jenna. When you shower, I'll take off the chain but I'll have to lock you in the bathroom." He smiled again. "Just for now, you understand?"

Emma felt she had no choice but to understand. To confront the man was unwise to the extreme. She nodded.

When Emma entered the tiny bathroom, she was surprised to find it well-designed, immaculately clean and utterly devoid of any means of escape. She stood on the toilet and looked out the small window set high on the wall. She breathed a sigh of disappointment. The window itself was too small for her to slither through and, to make things even worse, it was covered with bars.

By the stingy pre-dawn light Emma reconnoitered the area outside the window. It appeared the one-room stone and wood cabin was set towards the front of an oblong clearing. There was a small shed set on its right side. Dark, forbidding woods defined the perimeter of the cleared area as far as she could see. An almost invisible set of parallel tire tracks disappeared into the woods behind the shed.

# Chapter 16

Although a lot of people were doing a lot of work – they were not really any closer to finding Emma by Monday.

Early that morning, Caleb returned to work. He touched base with the Edmond Police, but there had been no new developments. The Chief had not yet received the results from the liquid found in the cup in Emma's car – still nothing on the fingerprint search. They'd identified Emma's prints, of course, and were in the process of obtaining fingerprint samples from Emma's roommate, friends, and professors in order to eliminate them from the mix.

Exhausted, as much from worry as lack of sleep, Caleb slumped into his desk chair. Deputy Sable sauntered up and perched on the corner of Caleb's desk. He looked at the undersheriff solemnly, "Hey, man, we're sorry to hear about Jenny's sister. You know if there's anything we can do...." He trailed off.

"Thanks, deputy. We're doing everything we can think of right now, but thanks."

Sable waited a moment and then said, "You hear O'Donnell got a job in D.C.? She's already out of here – gone just like that," he snapped his fingers. "She stopped in for a minute to say goodbye to everyone, but you weren't here." Sable surreptitiously scrutinized Caleb's body language for reactions.

Caleb knew exactly what Sable was doing. The new deputy was gossip-central for the entire office – maybe the whole damn state. The little prick had his nose into everything.

"Damned if I'll give him anything to talk about," Caleb thought. Aloud he said, "Hey, that's really great. I wish her the best of luck."

Sable nodded; obviously disappointed his news hadn't elicited a more dramatic response. As he got up to leave, he added, "Oh, before I forget.....I haven't been able to track down those tag numbers yet." Caleb looked back at him, obviously not understanding the reference. Sable continued, "You know, Sheriff Holcomb asked me to track down the tag numbers you got off the truck and trailer - when you and O'Donnell were out on cattle rustling surveillance?"

"Oh yeah – nothing on that yet?"

"Nope. Nobody's turned up squat."

"Well, keep at it." Caleb turned to review several new missing person reports that had come in overnight, but none of them appeared to fit.

**\*\*\*\*\*\*\*\*\*\***

Jenny re-read all the reports, lists, summarized activities – anything she could think of, but she, too, felt all they were doing was spinning their wheels.

Caleb, Jenny and Matt were sitting at the kitchen table picking at the meal Anna brought over when the phone rang. Caleb ran to answer. It was Chief Bauman.

"Caleb, I just got a call from Nathan Phillips with the OSBI. They have identified the liquid as GHB – a well-known date rape drug – and they are declaring Emma's disappearance as a kidnapping. Officially, the OSBI is taking over the case."

**\*\*\*\*\*\*\*\*\*\***

True to his word, on Tuesday afternoon Dr. Adams emailed the Tallchiefs a list of other meeting sites for the grief seminar. Matt and his mother composed and sent emails outlining what had happened to Emma and asking for any information about similar occurrences at their locations. It took most of the afternoon and evening to get them all sent.

Unsure as to where to go next, Matt proposed he drive to each of the grief seminar locations in Oklahoma and see if he could get any information. Caleb urged Matt to wait – see if they got any promising responses from their emails. But Matt would not be put off. He needed to physically do something – not just sit around sending emails and hoping someone might answer.

Caleb recognized Matt's need for action, so he agreed that Matt should drive to Durant – closest location to Tecumseh – to talk to the people at the church and see what he could find out. Truthfully, Caleb held out little hope Matt would find out anything useful – but at least it would keep Matt busy and out from underfoot.

"Matt, this is a real long shot," Caleb cautioned. "Don't expect too much. Why don't you try to get some sleep and start out first thing in the morning?"

Matt just grabbed his coat and headed out the door. If he had to, he'd knock on every door – harass every minister, associate minister or janitor – no matter what time it was. He'd camp out on the church steps – anything - until he got something. He didn't – couldn't – wait to find Emma. He was worried sick that no matter how quickly he moved - it may not be in time.

**********

Matt arrived in Durant, Oklahoma, well after 2:00 am Wednesday morning. The small city was fast asleep. There was no doubt the phrase "rolled up the sidewalks after dark" applied here.

Matt drove around the area several times, finally locating the small nondenominational church on Dr.

Adams' list about two miles south of the city center, toward Calera. It was a prefab metal structure with no adornments and only a small hand painted sign with the name "Living Today Church," the schedule of church services and a phone number written in block letters. There were no lights in or around the building and no living souls to be seen. Matt called the phone number, but the call went directly to voice mail.

Matt pulled into the parking lot determined to wait. He would be there when the church opened up first thing in the morning. Within five minutes, he was fast asleep.

**********

A banging on the car window three hours later abruptly brought Matt back to the land of the living. One of the patrolmen from Bryan County Sheriff's Office stood beside Matt's old blue pickup, shining his light onto Matt's sleep-worn face.

"Good morning, sir. Can I see some ID?" Matt cranked down his window and pulled his drivers license from his wallet as he rubbed the sleep from his eyes.

"How about vehicle registration?" Matt complied and handed over the vehicle registration from the glove box. The patrolman carefully reviewed the license and leaned in. "You any relation to Caleb Tallchief in Shawnee?"

Matt replied, "Yeah, he's my older brother."

"This about the posting on the list serve – um – his missing sister?"

"Yeah, actually it's his wife's sister, Emma Cochran. She went missing last Thursday night and we're all out looking for her. Truthfully," Matt admitted, "the OSBI is officially in charge of the case, but they're telling us squat. We're trying to track down any clues we can think of on our own – sort of as an independent inquiry."

The patrolman moved the light beam from Matt's face and shut it off. "Yeah, that Oklahoma City bunch is tight-assed and less than helpful. Don't really want to let us ignorant poor country folks in – we might actually find out something. We had a couple of cases with them over the years and they didn't exactly win any prizes for interagency cooperation, if you know what I mean."

The officer paused, "How can I help?"

Matt rubbed his eyes to clear the vestiges of sleep. "Last year this church," he gestured towards the Living Today Church building, "offered the same grief seminar as the one Emma disappeared from."

"We thought – well, I thought - I might be able to get something from the people at the church that would help us – maybe point us in some direction. Right now, we've got nothing."

The patrolman suggested Matt follow him to the Bryan County Sheriff's Office in Durant. He'd call some folks and maybe they could put their heads together and find something.

The officer must have called en route, because Sheriff Bill Tulley was already there when Matt pulled up to the station fifteen minutes later.

Tulley was exiting his vehicle carrying a bag of fresh donuts. "I know," he said, glancing at the bakery bag in his hand, "it's kind of a cliché, isn't it? But I do love donuts."

He continued, "I know Joe Holcolmb pretty well," Tulley said. "Haven't met your brother, but we heard about his rescue of that little girl a couple of months ago. That was really something."

"Yeah. Tell the truth; Cal was sort of embarrassed by all the hoopla. There was a town celebration and everything. He had to make a speech. I don't know that I've ever seen Caleb turn that particular shade of red before," he recalled.

Over coffee and donuts, Matt repeated the story he shared earlier with the patrolman. He explained the minister at Life Today Church in Edmond had given them a list of other churches that had hosted the same or a similar grief seminar. Matt was trying to get information whether any of their participants had gone missing, like Emma, or if anything out of the ordinary had occurred.

"Pretty thin, I know," said Matt. "But right now we're grasping at straws."

"Well, I know the minister of Living Today Church. It's a pretty small congregation – probably don't have more than thirty members, I'd guess. The Baptist and

Methodist Churches reign supreme here. The Living Today Church minister isn't even full time. He owns a small antique shop over on Main Street, and I don't think he goes out to the church every day. Not sure if they even have a secretary. Let's wait a couple of hours and then I'll give him a call."

Matt wasn't entirely comfortable with waiting, but he bowed to the wisdom of the Sheriff. He certainly didn't want to alienate any possible information source and the Sheriff could be a Godsend in paving the way for the minister's cooperation.

In small towns, it's who you knew – not who you were that mattered. Outsiders needed someone to vouch for them if they hoped to get anywhere at all. And, who better to do the vouching than the Sheriff – at least among law-abiding residents.

"So tell me about this grief seminar," Tulley leaned forward for a sip of his stiff black coffee and another donut.

"From what I understand, it's designed to help people cope with the loss of close family members. For those who are primarily left alone. To help them with the emotional problem of being all alone," Matt explained.

"So, why was your – why was Emma – at this Edmond seminar? She's got family."

"We just don't know. But we do know she was attending."

"Okay. I guess we'll just have to ask her when we find her."

Both men lapsed into a silence lasting several minutes. Tulley broke it by saying, "You know, we don't have a lot of people go missing from around here - except for those foreigners who go to Southeastern. They come and go and nobody can keep up with them." He gave Matt a knowing look.

"But I do remember a case from last year – maybe a year and half now – her name's Marcy Ford. Her going missing was kind of the last act in a tragic play, you know? She was all alone, too – like you were saying about the people in this church seminar. Her mom and daddy lived up north of Armstrong on a small farm. She was their only child."

He continued, "Remember that big flood we had about two years back– the one where the Blue River ran a mile out of its banks?"

Matt nodded.

"Well, they, Marcy's parents, was both killed in that flood. Swept away – just like that." He snapped his fingers for emphasis.

"The 180th Guard unit was called in to help with the flood, evacuating, and relocating people, and they was the ones who found the Ford's SUV about three miles downstream – both parents drowned inside."

"Marcie was going to Southeastern when they died. It was real sad. She was real tore up about it. The town, too. Her family had been here for generations. There were so many people at their funeral; the Baptist Church had to rent chairs from the Methodists. Probably one of the few times those two groups ever worked together."

"Then when Marcy came up missing – it was her roommate filed the report. I guess there wasn't anyone else left," he mused.

Tulley fell silent for another minute or two. Matt sipped his coffee.

The Sheriff continued, "After looking for some time, we just plain ran out of places to look or people to talk to. Never found hide nor hair of that girl. We figured she went away – too many memories of her family to stay around here. Maybe we were wrong."

Sheriff Tulley got up and shuffled around in a metal cabinet behind his desk. He pulled out a file and opened it to reveal several typewritten pages along with several photos. He turned the file so that Matt could see the pictures inside. Matt couldn't believe it.

Physically, Marcy and Emma could have been sisters.

\*\*\*\*\*\*\*\*\*\*

Later that morning, Tulley introduced Matt to Floyd Miller, owner of Texoma Jewelry & Antiques, and minister of Living Today Church. Texoma Jewelry & Antiques was located in one of the original brick and stone buildings lining Main Street. It had the expected large glass display windows facing the street with a green solid wood door dividing the store front. Inside, glass-enclosed jewelry cases ran down either side and across the back of the first floor. There was a mezzanine above with access staircases on both the right and left hand sides of the main floor. The balcony housed the store's "antiques."

Miller's office was a large table located in the center back of the second floor. It was from this location, the small, slender, slightly-balding man orchestrated his jewelry, antique, and spiritual businesses. The Reverend Miller motioned for the two men to ascend the stairs when they entered at the front of the store.

Stairs groaned painfully as the two men climbed to the second floor. "The antique business must be very good," thought Matt as he threaded his way through the dusty, cluttered aisle, "or it must be very bad. Wonder if Miller has ever sold anything from up here?"

The three men gathered around Miller's 'desk.' The Reverend offered coffee, and both Matt and Tulley politely accepted.

"I don't know that I can help you, Sheriff. You know, church business is pretty confidential. Besides, the seminar you're asking about took place more'n a year and a half ago."

As their host poured each man a steaming mug of what appeared to be black tar, Matt looked around the space. He spied the photo of a young man dressed in desert camouflage combat gear. The uniform sported a Thunderbird insignia on its sleeve. Matt picked up the photo. "Your son?" he asked.

"Yes," Miller responded proudly. "He's with the 180th Guard unit here in Durant. You know him?"

"No, but I just got back from Afghanistan, and I met some of the 180th while they were deployed. I don't believe I met your son."

"Jim's there right now. Too bad you didn't meet up. He's a wonderful person. You'd have liked each other, I think." Matt replaced the photo in its original spot.

After the exchange, Miller seemed a little less reserved – a little more willing to talk to the two men. He stood up and went to an ancient file cabinet. The drawer hung up when Miller tugged at it, but he was finally able to extricate a slender folder. He opened it as he sat down and turned the folder so its contents could be shared.

Tulley showed him a photo of Marcy Ford.

"Yes, I remember Marcy. She'd lost her folks in that big flood of the Blue. She was really shaken up by it – in what you might call a 'crisis of faith.' Her folks had always been very religious – good solid Baptists. But Marcy didn't seem to be getting too much comfort from the church folks, so she was looking for help elsewhere."

"Did anything odd happen at any of the sessions?"

"No, there were only five – maybe six – people attending. Of course, there was a lot of sharing of grief stories. A lot of emotional outpouring – but then that's what you'd expect and even hope for at this type of seminar. It gives people a chance to voice their pain – maybe help get it out of their system. There was one young man who'd just lost his mother to cancer. He was especially traumatized. He and Marcy sat together at most of the meetings."

Matt asked, "Do you remember anything odd that happened – before or after any of the sessions? Any angry words in the parking lot – something like that?"

The Reverend replied. "No, I can't recall anything out of the ordinary."

"Did Marcy miss any of the group meetings?"

"No, she attended every one."

"Do you think Marcy was likely to just up and leave the area without telling anyone?"

Reverend Miller considered the question for a long moment. "Yes, I heard Marcy went missing not long after the seminar ended. I thought it odd at the time. Even though I didn't know her all that well, that behavior just didn't seem to go along with what I saw in her. I remember the young woman as being very caring – she provided a shoulder to cry on for a couple of the others. Truthfully, she seemed to be adapting to her loss better than most. She was sad – but not devastated or suicidal."

"Would you happen to have the names and addresses of the people who attended your seminar? The man Marcy sat with? Any information would help," asked Matt.

"We didn't keep a roster – the seminar literature suggested we only ask for first names and a short synopsis of the trauma the person had. The designers of the seminar said people wouldn't feel so exposed that way. We did as was suggested. So I don't have last names or addresses."

"But I'll ask around some of the church members to see if I can find out anything for you," Miller promised. "Don't hold out too much hope, though, the seminar was quite a while ago. People move on."

Even though the Reverend couldn't provide a lot of details, Matt was elated – he finally had a connection. Two women of the same physical description had attended grief seminars and had subsequently disappeared.

**********

Matt called Caleb with the news and Caleb hurried to put the new information out to his colleagues across the state. Hopefully, they'd get more hits. Caleb also shared the information with Fred Johnson at the University and the Edmond police chief. The Edmond police chief promised to pass the information along to the OSBI.

Not sure where to go from here, Matt decided to head home, hoping something would pop from Caleb's new postings. He was pumped – even though he was not quite sure how this new information would help. At least it was something.

As Matt got into his pickup to leave, Tulley approached the driver's side door. "Matt, I want to apologize to you and your brother. I should have put these two cases together."

Matt replied, "Sheriff Tulley there was no way you could have known Emma's and Marcy's disappearances might be linked. It was only when we looked at their photos and talked to Reverend Miller that we knew something was up."

"I want you to know I'm going to re-interview everybody associated with Marcy Ford's disappearance. If anything comes up, I'll let you and Caleb know right away."

The two men shook hands. Matt shut the door to his old blue pickup, cranked up his heater, and headed north.

**********

Caleb and Jenny, too, had been busy. They decided to revisit and talk to anyone who might know something about the nine cases they had deemed as priority from the missing person reports. They opted for in-person interviews rather than phone calls or emails, because one never knew what off-hand comment or nuance might provide a critical clue.

The first on their list was Sarah Metheny, reported missing a year ago from Christian Brothers College, located in Muskogee, Oklahoma. Caleb had made an appointment for Jenny and himself with the College Registrar for early Wednesday morning.

When Caleb stepped from his SUV, he thought he had stepped back in time. The campus was tiny – it probably could have housed no more than 200 students. There were six old buildings covered in ivy in the most traditional of campus settings.

The students, too, looked as though they belonged to a different era. They were well-dressed – not a pair of jeans, pajamas, or a skateboard in sight - no blue or pink spiked hair. More astonishingly, the young people appeared to be respectful of Caleb's uniform. One young man personally guided the two to the Administration Building. Maybe college was like this during the 1950's, but it sure wasn't like the University either Caleb or Jenny attended.

The Registrar, Ms. Adelaide Barstow, also seemed from a different era. She was elderly, prim, and adorned with the requisite round rimless spectacles.

Although sympathetic to their situation, she didn't think she could help. The student in question had indeed been reported missing by her major advisor, Dr. Green, but subsequent to that report, the student had been found. The registrar had duly reported her findings to the local authorities at the time

Although Ms. Barstow provided no specific facts, her obvious careful choice of words left no doubt that the unfortunate Ms. Metheny had been found in rather personally compromising circumstances. The Registrar confirmed Ms. Metheny was not currently a student at Christian Brothers College. Her tone made it perfectly clear the young woman would never again be accepted as a student at Christian Brothers College.

The Tallchiefs walked inconsolably back to the PottCo Sheriff's Office SUV. Disappointed with their lack of progress, Jenny yanked open the passenger door, and angrily threw her purse into the seat. In the same instant Jenny's purse hit the front seat, the bushes on the far side of the sidewalk rattled. A small white puppy emerged and dashed across the concrete. It leaped into the truck door opening and flopped down onto the floorboard as far away from the door as it could get.

Jenny's expression softened. "Well, hi there, little one. I don't think you want to go with us," Jenny reached down to pick up the puppy and as she touched it, she sensed its fear and its pain.

Almost immediately, an old black beat-up pickup shrieked to a stop beside the SUV. The slogan "Pets for You" was emblazoned in poor hand-painted lettering on the side of the driver's door. A rough-looking middle-aged man threw open his door, jumped out, and confronted Jenny. Jenny could have sworn she smelled alcohol on his breath from the second he exited his truck.

"Hey, you seen a puppy? White, curly hair?" he demanded, moving into Jenny's personal space and assuming a threatening posture. Jenny thought he'd probably seen the little animal jump into Jenny's truck.

Before Caleb could speak, Jenny brought herself up to her full 5' 1" height, looked the barrel-chested bully straight in the eye, and responded sharply, "No, no - we haven't. Mr...... What did you say your name is? Are you from around here? ?" Jenny glanced at the truck. "Do you own a licensed pet shop?"

A light went on behind the man's angry red-rimmed eyes. Fear replaced the belligerence. He stepped back out of Jenny's space and edged back toward his truck's open door.

"Uh, ..... Smith. Mr. Smith." Apparently, "Mr. Smith" had just realized Jenny and Caleb were in a sheriff's vehicle and Caleb, now fully visible on the far side of the SUV was wearing a law enforcement uniform.

As Caleb circled around the black pickup, he noticed several animal crates beneath a tarp thrown across the top and took mental note of the license tag number.

Mr. Smith backed up a few more steps. It was obvious he didn't want anything to do with this couple. Uh, thanks." He hurriedly jumped into his pickup, backed out and sped away as fast as he thought he could get away with.

Jenny watched him go with anger in her eyes. "Caleb, that is one bad man. What do you want to bet he runs a puppy mill not far from here?"

Jenny leaned back into the SUV. "No way was I

going to let him have this little baby." Jenny picked up the small terrified animal and held it close.

Caleb got on his radio and contacted the sheriff's office. He gave them the license number of the pick-up and relayed his concerns that this man might be into something not quite kosher – perhaps a puppy mill. With all the negative publicity the area had seen lately regarding animal abuse – especially cock fighting and puppy mills, he was sure "Mr. Smith's" activities would be investigated thoroughly.

# Chapter 17

"John, I really need to go into town," Emma stated matter-of-factly.

"Why's that? You've got everything you need here," John smiled at Emma.

"Well, these clothes are getting pretty rank. And, even though I can wash them in the sink, I don't have anything to wear while they dry."

"Not a problem, Jenna. There are some spare clothes in that old chest right there at the foot of the bed. Just pick out whatever you like."

Emma walked across the room, her chain making clinking sounds as it dragged along the wood and across the small rug in front of the fireplace. She opened the lid of the trunk and found it divided into two sections. On the right side were men's jeans, shirts, underwear and socks. On the left were some worn pairs of women's jeans, a couple of shirts and some socks. There were also several pair of panties. All the items appeared to be just about her size.

"John, whose clothes are these?"

John's demeanor underwent an immediate transformation. Gone was the smiling, tolerant loving man. In his place was a stranger – the man who had briefly made himself known during their journey to the cabin. Anger flashed from his eyes.

"Don't you worry, little miss. Those clothes are yours now. They'll fit you just fine. Just wear them and don't ask any questions."

# Chapter 18

For Caleb and Jenny, the next two missing person interviews were as unproductive as the first. Both missing girls had been subsequently located, but the official police records had not been updated. One was working in a local beauty shop – having determined the traditional college route was not for her - and the second had been found in a ravine – the apparent victim of a one-car accident.

************

On Thursday, Jenny, Caleb and Jesse set out for Ada, Oklahoma, to meet with their police chief, Sam Gilley. Gilley had shared with Sheriff Holcomb information about a missing person case he had handled six months ago. Holcomb thought it might be worth Caleb's time to go see what the man had to say.

Gilley welcomed the Tallchiefs, shaking hands and offering coffee. He knew they were worried sick about Emma, so he got right to his story.

Last spring a young woman, attending East Central University, had been reported missing by her boyfriend. She'd been gone for a couple of days. The boyfriend thought she'd gone off in a snit after they'd had an argument, but when she failed to return to their shared apartment after a few days – he reported it to the campus police. The campus cops had, in turn, notified the Ada Police Department.

The young woman had taken her purse and car, but only the clothes she was wearing. Her bank account hadn't been touched – not that she had that much in it. According to University records, she'd quit going to class, but hadn't officially withdrawn. Her college records didn't show any next of kin, so it didn't appear she went back home to her family. She simply vanished.

The chief had looked seriously at the boyfriend, but could find no evidence to indicate the disappearance was a result of foul play – much less foul play by the young man living with the missing girl. On the contrary, by the accounts of the couple's friends, the two generally got along very well.

The case went cold about a month later. There was just no one else to talk to nor were there any new leads.

Then, about a month ago, one of the Ada city

patrolmen made a routine traffic stop. The driver bolted and tried to run, but the patrolman ran faster.

The man turned out to be a legal resident alien from Mexico. The chief had had his eyes on this guy for some time – suspected him of drug dealing on the East Central campus, but could never get any evidence on him. This time, however, they could get him – not on drugs, but on car theft. The car he was driving was registered to their missing person.

Even though nothing in the initial missing person investigation revealed the victim had any connection to drugs, the current line of thinking was that she had gotten crosswise with these drug dealers and wound up in real trouble. The kind of trouble that caused a person to disappear, either voluntarily or in a box.

According to the photos in her file, Stephanie Rushing was a petite blonde.

**********

Caleb got a call from Sheriff Holcomb as he, Jenny and Jesse drove north toward Shawnee. The Sheriff asked Caleb to report to the office as soon as he got back to town. Caleb dropped Jenny and the dog off at home and continued on to Shawnee.

Caleb was met with raised eyebrows and inquiring looks as he entered the building. Sheriff Holcomb stuck his head out of his office door and gestured for Caleb to join him.

Inside the office, Caleb found the Sheriff behind his desk and two men in suits sitting in the chairs facing the Sheriff. They stood when Caleb entered, extending their hands in a gesture of friendship and cooperation. Caleb had made them for OSBI the second he set eyes on them.

The taller of the two men – the one obviously in charge – began. "Officer Tallchief, first let us say how sorry we are about your sister's disappearance."

Caleb held up his hand as if to ward off any further insincere commiserations. "First, it's Undersheriff Tallchief. And second, it's my sister-in-law. Obviously, you haven't been sorry enough to read the file."

"Back off, Caleb," interjected the Sheriff. He eyed the two visitors. "Just say what you came to say and let's be done with it."

"Okay, if that's the way you want to play it," the OSBI investigator's eyes hardened into a cold glare directed straight at Caleb. His words sounded as though they were being read from a card.

"This is a formal visit to inform you that the OSBI has deemed Emma Cochran's disappearance a kidnapping. The OSBI is officially in charge of this investigation and we will tolerate no interference from any local or rural agencies."

He continued, "We know you've been off playing the cowboy – investigating on your own. You are now officially being ordered to cease any further investigation. Any information you have in your possession should be forwarded immediately to my attention."

He handed the Sheriff his card. "Our office will request and share information as it deems appropriate."

The two men collected their overcoats and exited the Sheriff's Office without further comment.

# Chapter 19

Later that evening, Jenny walked up to the counter at Ellie's Deli & Café and ordered ten specials to go.

Although Ellie was up-to-date in many of her business practices, she was not yet enlightened enough to let dogs into her cafe. So Jesse sat on her haunches outside on the sidewalk and waited patiently.

Jenny hadn't bothered to read the sandwich board menu outside the door, so she had no idea what today's special was. It didn't really matter. The food was just fuel for another brainstorming session; however, this time the brains belonged to professional law enforcement people.

The restaurant was about half full, although Ellie was probably not making very much money from her clientele. The tables, covered with red checked cloths, and the red vinyl-covered booths were occupied by the "old guys." They sat in small groups eating snacks, drinking coffee or just spinning tales, as they did most every evening. A couple of years ago in an effort to cut costs, Ellie had tried to close her business right after the lunch rush. However, she met with such infuriated protests from her "regulars" – some even threatened to boycott her establishment – that Ellie wisely and immediately returned to her old schedule. Now she just chalked up the evening's low profit margin to involuntary community service.

As Jenny entered the restaurant, chatter ceased and heads turned in her direction. They all knew who she was, of course, and they also knew Emma was missing. This recent misfortune - added to Jenny's earlier run-in with the convicts and Caleb's rescue of Lindsay Ann - had made the Tallchiefs the primary source of Tecumseh gossip for the last several months. Jenny would not be surprised if the old geezers knew every detail of Emma's investigation so far. Maybe she should ask them where Emma was.

Several of the "old geezers" nodded in greeting, but most did not acknowledge Jenny's presence. After all, though the Tallchief family was one of their own, Jenny and her sister were still "outsiders." One had to live in town much, much longer to be considered a true member of "the community" – even if one married into the group.

This attitude apparently did not apply to all those seated about the room, as one of the old guys quickly came to his feet and hurried over to Jenny.

"Any news?" Joe Tallchief asked.

"No, Joe, nothing. We're running down leads and got some information, but nothing seems to point us to Emma yet. You know the OSBI has been called in. They found a date rape drug in the coffee cup residue we found in Emma's car. Her case is now officially a kidnapping. The OSBI hasn't told us anything yet – in fact, they told us to butt out." Jenny sounded despondent.

"Come sit with us while you wait for your order," he urged.

Ellie agreed. "It's going to take a few minutes to put this together, honey," she told Jenny gently.

Jenny followed Joe to a table and found Paul White Horse sitting there, sipping a cup of steaming coffee. Joe brought over two more - one for himself and one for Jenny. The three discussed the lack of progress in finding Emma.

Paul White Horse looked intently at Jenny and said sternly, "You must get some order – some calm back in your mind."

Jenny had had enough. "How can I possibly do that?" she snapped. "Besides you were the one who told me I had to hurry."

"That is true. But I also said you had to listen, to trust, and to communicate. You can't do any of those things if your mind is full of anger and fear. You must clear your mind of emotions that suck the spirit from you - for they will shout above all else and you will be consumed."

Having spoken those words of doom which conveyed

absolutely nothing of use to Jenny, Paul began the laborious process of filling and lighting his pipe.

Jenny's temper was one micrometer from pulling a Mount St. Helen's. Paul White Horse was just plain nuts.

She breathed a sign of relief when, just then, Ellie called her name with her order. "Good timing," she thought. "I might have had to hurt that old man."

Jenny paid and headed quickly out the door, her thoughts and emotions tumbling over one another. "What in the hell did he expect from her? How could she possibly 'clear her mind?' To hear what – the wind moaning a message? The trees writing in the dirt with their branches? Good God."

Joe caught up with her outside. "Jenny, don't be angry with Paul. He sees things very differently than we do. He's a Seminole spiritual leader, you know, like a medicine man. He's always been a little out there," Joe paused, "but he's also been right more times than not. I wouldn't discount what he has to say."

"I know, Joe, Jenny replied. "But he says things that make no sense. All that woojie-woojie stuff – that doesn't help at all."

She looked at Joe. He was only trying to help. After all, Emma was his family, too. "I'm sorry, Joe. We're just at our wits end right now. We don't know what to do next. Nothing seems to help us find her. She's been gone almost a week now. I know in my heart she's alive, but if we don't find her soon – we may never find her."

**********

Sitting around the Tallchief kitchen table were Matt, Sheriff Holcomb, and Fred Johnson. Fred Johnson and Sheriff Holcolmb had volunteered to help the Tallchiefs organize the search for Emma – even though the case was now officially in the hands of the OSBI.

Caleb was standing in front of a white board and busily outlining all the facts they had thus far collected. He turned from the board as the kitchen door opened and Jenny and Jesse blew in on a blast of freezing November air – food bags in arm.

Fred Johnson jumped to his feet to help Jenny and Holcomb took drink orders. No sooner had the contents of the Styrofoam containers been piled high on paper plates than another brisk knock shook the back door.

Caleb opened it to find Chief Mike Bauman shivering in the spotlight over the back porch. Much to Caleb's surprise, the OSBI agent from that afternoon's meeting – the one who had not spoken – stepped out from behind Bauman and onto the porch.

"What the hell…"

Caleb didn't get the whole sentence out before Fred Johnson moved up behind Caleb and said, "I invited Mike. I thought the more brains and experience we dump into the mix – the better."

"And, I," continued Bauman, "invited Special Agent

169

Eric McBride. He and I have been good friends since high school – even though he wound up in the OSBI."

Caleb drew in a breath to speak, but Bauman held up his hand and continued, "Eric thinks the OSBI completely missed the mark by excluding you in this investigation. He'll be able to help and can fill us in on what the OSBI learns. I hope you guys don't mind."

The icy air sweeping into the kitchen from the open door wasn't the only reason the room had turned frigid. Caleb and Holcomb, still stinging from that afternoon's OSBI rebuke, turned to Agent McBride.

"No way you're getting in here. You don't give a shit about finding Emma – you just want to make sure we don't find her first," argued Caleb.

McBride answered, "Look, I'm sorry for the way this afternoon went. I told Jack Storey, my partner, that we were stupid to exclude you all," he nodded to the group around the table. "I told him you could probably find out more in one day than we could in a week. In fact, I argued so strongly, I almost got myself kicked off the case."

As Holcomb and Caleb stood eye-to-eye with Bauman and McBride, Jesse quietly inserted herself between the two sets of antagonists. She grasped the OSBI Agent by the coat sleeve and led him to an empty chair at the table.

She turned her deep brown eyes on the three men still standing in the open doorway, as if to say, "Turn down the testosterone, boys. We need all the help we can get."

Astonished, Holcomb looked at Caleb and said, "Well, I guess that settles that."

**\*\*\*\*\*\*\*\*\*\***

Matt, Caleb and Jenny reviewed the facts they had uncovered – the two missing women and the grief seminar. They added conjectures, thoughts and perceptions as they were voiced by others around the table to the big whiteboard.

When they had listed everything they knew or thought they knew or guessed they knew, they had finished all the food and the drinks, but were no closer to finding Emma.

All agreed there was no way these incidents could be unconnected. They most assuredly were dealing with a serial kidnapper. And, since none of the women had ever reappeared, they also assumed they were dealing with a serial murderer.

# Chapter 20

Several days had passed since Emma's arrival at the cabin. John had not left her side – except to use the bathroom or bring in more firewood. He had been so overly solicitous she wanted to scream. He carefully prepared her meals and constantly asked after her well-being. He kept her chained to the fireplace, and no amount of cajoling on Emma's part could convince him to release her. She had even begun to whine about the cuff's irritation to her ankle skin. Tyler handed her a pair of thick socks.

John slept each night in the big brown leather recliner, leaving the bed for Emma alone. He pulled the chair close to Emma so they wouldn't be far apart. He explained that it wouldn't be right for them to share a bed until they were man and wife officially. But when that happened, he was sure the single bed would be just fine for the two of them.

Then again, he told her, when they were married,

they would most likely move into the big house in the family compound near Harley. After all, that's where his father and brothers lived with their families. That way, Jenna would have the other wives to talk to and she wouldn't be lonely when John was away on business. He had it all planned out.

John talked extensively about his mother, how much he had loved her. He told her his mom had not died of cancer as he had led the participants in the seminar to believe – rather she had died in a car wreck.

"Some people around here thought my father had something to do with her accident," John said, "but I know for a fact he loved her completely. He would never – never have hurt a hair on her head. He did make her toe the line, though."

Truthfully, John could remember several times he had witnessed his father beat his mother mercilessly – but that was not how he would treat his wife. There would be no need, as he was sure Jenna would be much more obedient and respectful than his mother ever was.

John quickly changed the subject. He asked, "Jenna, why do you wear that big ring with the "E" on it? I see you looking at it from time to time. Your name starts with a "J"."

Emma panicked. She had to think quickly. Thank God her gift for fantasy had not eluded her, "Uh, John. My mother's name began with an "E" – Emma. I wear it for her."

John nodded in understanding and patted Emma's hand as if to console her. "Yes, we both really loved our mothers, didn't we?"

\*\*\*\*\*\*\*\*\*\*

Friday morning dawned cold and grey. Mist hung low over the clearing and the trees beyond were invisible under a suspended blanket of gloom. John was up early, bringing in more wood and stoking the fire up to a healthy crackle and pop. Even though John covered the woodpile with a heavy tarp, some of last night's freezing rain had wormed its way into the logs. He started the coffee and its pleasant aroma wafted its way across the cabin's interior and tickled Emma's nostrils.

"Wake up, sleepy head," Tyler urged. "You really have to quit sleeping so much. I'm beginning to think you sleep just to avoid me." John smiled, but there was an edge to his voice.

Emma startled and opened her eyes. How had he known? Or was he just guessing? It was uncanny – the way this man could inveigle his way into her mind and pick out her thoughts.

She, in fact, had been awake for hours – her mind racing. She thought about the clue she'd left with that boy at the grocery store and prayed it would make its way to Jenny. But, Emma thought despondently, even then – how would Jenny find her way out here in the middle of nowhere? If she was to get free, she'd have to do it on her own.

John brought Emma some steaming coffee – with lots of milk – just like she liked it. He pulled the recliner closer to the bed and sat down so he could look at Emma right in the eyes.

His voice became very serious. "I have some work to do today, Jenna. Some people to meet with, so you need to stay here by yourself."

Emma was thrilled, even though she willed her expression to show disappointment. Perhaps she could find some way out of this place if she had some time without John's constant surveillance.

"So," she whined. "Will you be away all day?"

"Well, I do have a lot to do, so I probably won't be back until early evening. But I promise I'll be home before it gets really dark so you won't have to be afraid. Okay, Jenna?"

"I guess – if you really have to go."

"I'll be as quick as I can. And maybe I'll even bring you a special treat when I come back." John smiled at Jenna like a tolerant father.

John continued. "Now Jenna. Here's the rules. It's very important you mind me on this. Okay, you understand? Don't try to get out of your ankle chain. It's there for your protection. We're getting along real good now. It won't be long before I can really trust you – but you try to get away and, well, I won't be able to trust you any longer, will I?" John smiled at the implied threat.

Emma stared at him.

"Good. Now, another thing. You stay away from that desk." He gestured to the roll top sequestered in the far corner of the room. "It's none of your business. It's man's work – not anything for you to worry about. There's food in the refrigerator and some magazines for you to read."

As John left, Emma noticed that the fog had begun to lift. "Good," she thought. "It'll be easier for me to find my way out of here."

Emma waited impatiently for about an hour after John had left the cabin. She didn't want him to walk in on her banging at the fireplace or sawing at her ankle chain.

She began experimenting on how she could free herself. She first examined the chain's attachment to the fireplace. She pried away at it with knives and the worn hammer she found in the kitchen toolbox, but after an hour of unrewarded effort, she determined the chain's end was solidly embedded into the mortar and stone – not a chance she could get it loose. Then she swept up the evidence – the mortar chips and other debris - and threw them into the blazing fire. Further experimentation with the ankle cuff yielded no better results.

She tackled the kitchen next. She went through every drawer in the kitchen and then the bathroom looking for the key to the cuff – or anything she could use to free herself. She knew John had taken a key with him, but she hoped against hope there might be a duplicate.

When, after hours of exploration and experimentation, nothing seemed to work, Emma banged her fists in frustration on the kitchen's countertop. Tears of desperation flooded down her face. "Knock it off, Emma. Knock it off. You've got to think." She told herself.

"Nothing. There's just nothing…." Emma's eyes fell on the forbidden desk.

Emma retrieved a small flathead screwdriver from the tool box. She gently pried at the lock on the roll top desk until she heard a metallic click. Unfortunately, the metallic sound was accompanied by the crack of wood.

"Oh, shit. How can I hide this?" But the thought of hiding the damage from the break-in quickly gave way to her need to find a key for the ankle cuff – and find it quick. She had to get free and away from this lunatic as soon as she could.

She quickly opened and closed each drawer – searched each cubbyhole – but found no key. When Emma pulled open the bottom drawer on the right hand side of the desk, she found a small metal box.

She slowly lifted the container from its hiding place and placed it in the center of the desk. Her hands shook as she pried it open.

"In for a penny – in for a pound," she thought as

she worked on the container. She slowly opened the lid, but to her disappointment – she found no key – only some driver's licenses, two necklaces and several rings. Emma turned over the licenses and the jewelry in her hand – what were these things? Why did John have them?

The truth hit her like a sledgehammer. "Oh my God," she said aloud. "These are trophies! These are remembrances from other women he has kept here."

And now she understood why the worn clothes from the chest fit her so well. Each of the driver's licenses' physical description was a match to her. The clothes had belonged to them.

Emma sat back and stared at the licenses – not moving, barely breathing. At some primordial level she knew John had killed these women. She also knew he would kill her, too.

Emma heard John's truck pull to a stop outside the cabin. He had apparently finished his "work" early. She had been concentrating so hard on finding a means of escape, she had lost track of time and hadn't noticed the late afternoon shadows lengthening across the clearing. Stupid – stupid! How could she have been so stupid?

Emma swiftly replaced the box's contents and closed the desk top. She had barely enough time to slide into the big leather recliner in front of the fireplace and pick up a magazine when the icy blast of cold air announcing John's arrival filled the room.

Emma rose from the chair and tried to appear

nonchalant. She asked about his day, and John answered noncommitantly. John could sense that Emma was hiding something – something he would not like. Emma intentionally avoided looking at the desk, keeping her eyes on John or the fire.

He handed Emma some new magazines – mostly about home decorating, recipes and other domestic endeavors. She thanked him profusely and sat down to thumb through her gifts.

Tyler knew there was something amiss. He slowly scanned the room. The kitchen was just a little different than when he had left this morning, but Emma had probably fixed herself something to eat at some point today.

His eyes fell on his desk. Something was odd about the desk. He walked over to the corner and realized the lock had been broken. Although Emma had hurriedly tried to hide the damage she had done in prying up the roll top, she had obviously not been as successful as she had hoped.

"You been at this desk, ain't you?" John whirled on Emma.

"No, John. Honest…"

"Don't lie to me, woman." He strode across the room, pulled Emma to her feet and slapped her hard across the face.

"And we were getting along so well. I really thought you were the one – damnit, damnit." He hit her hard in the stomach and she stumbled and fell backwards on the floor.

"What did you find?" he asked in a low, menacing tone.

"Nothing – nothing." Emma's mind raced for an acceptable response. "I was looking for a key. I wanted to show you I would stay with you even if I didn't have the chain on."

"You stupid bitch. You've ruined everything!"

Emma knew he was going to kill her – just as he had killed the women whose licenses and jewelry she had found. She frantically searched her mind, hoping to find some way to stem his anger.

"John, I'm really sorry. I won't disobey you again. You're right – we are really good together…"

"Just shut up, will you? I've got to think. Get away from me, woman."

John jammed on his coat and went out into the late afternoon twilight. He flexed and unflexed his hands. He really wanted to beat her senseless, but he needed to think first – to sort things out. He didn't want to do anything he'd later regret. After all, he was a planner.

As he sat on the front porch watching the darkness creep in from the woods around him, John pondered his options. He really did love Jenna "– but she was a stupid untrustworthy bitch – just like the others." John sighed deeply. He couldn't risk it. She'd have to go. He was sure there would be another. A woman he could trust completely. One who would be perfect. He just had to keep looking. And, after all, that really wasn't so bad. He enjoyed the chase almost as much as the prize.

John Tyler sighed again, feeling betrayed and saddened. And convinced that his next actions were fully justified by Jenna's treachery.

He stomped across the clearing to the shed to get his shovel. As he entered the wooded area to the north of the cabin, Emma watched him from the window. She knew she was out of time.

# Chapter 21

After Jenny had calmed down a bit, she decided to take Paul White Horse's advice and try to inject a little normalcy into her routine in order to clear her mind.

Early Friday morning, she went into work at the clinic and was greeted by an avalanche of paperwork on her desk. She began by sorting and stacking the various reports, medical supply orders and telephone messages. As she put the telephone messages into date order, she noticed one of the callers had been particularly persistent about reaching her.

Curious, Jenny called in Annie Hawthorne.

"Annie, there are twenty-two messages here from a Mrs. Turney or Craig Turney. What's the deal?"

"Oh those," Annie's disdainful expression and dismissive tone left no doubt as to what she thought about those callers.

"I finally had to tell them to quit calling yesterday. They started early Saturday morning and on and on and on. There was even some calls from the service late Friday night and Sunday. I explained and explained to this crazy woman that Dr. Tallchief had a family emergency and was taking some time off and we didn't know for sure when you'd be in…. But this "person" would not take "NO" for an answer. Time and time again, she called until, finally I told her not to call back." Annie crossed her arms across her ample chest and slowly nodded once for emphasis.

"OK, thanks, Annie."

Annie turned, still on a roll about those phone calls. "Oh, my gosh, she was a real nut case. And that kid of hers – going on about a "honey cure" and that you were the only one who he could talk to. You'd think there wasn't another vet .."

"What did you say?"

"I said he thought you were the only vet on the face of this earth…"

"No," Jenny almost screamed. "What did you say about the "honey cure?"

"Well, I mean – enough is enough."

Jenny wanted to wring Annie's neck. "Tell me exactly word for word what they said."

"Well, she said a pretty young lady had told her grandson to get ahold of you about their dog who is pretty sick. The boy told his grandma to call Dr. Tallchief, the vet in Tecumseh, because that vet could for sure heal his dog with the "honey cure." She told the boy not to talk to anyone else – only Dr. Tallchief.

I told that crazy woman I never even heard of a honey cure…and no vet could ever for sure heal any animal and that Dr. Martin was the senior vet at this clinic anyway and he…"

"Annie, I need to make a phone call right now." Jenny's voice was low, but her tone left no doubt she was furious with the receptionist and about to erupt. She abruptly shoo'ed Annie away from her doorway and grabbed her phone.

Sounding miffed, probably because she hadn't yet finished her tirade, Annie responded, "Well, I'm needed up front anyhow." She turned and huffed out of the room.

Annie's response was only half-heard as Jenny tried to punch in the phone number on the message slip. After two attempts her shaking fingers finally got the number right and Jenny connected with Mrs. Turney. They spoke briefly and then Jenny snatched her vet bag and purse.

She ran out the Clinic's door, down the hallway and outside to her car without acknowledging Annie or any of the waiting patients at all.

"Well, I'll be. What's wrong with her?" was all Annie could think to say.

\*\*\*\*\*\*\*\*\*\*

Jenny didn't want to take the time to call Caleb

before heading his way and she didn't trust herself to call and drive at the same time. She sped the eight miles up Highway 177 from the Clinic to Shawnee as fast as humanly possible and came to a screeching halt in the Sheriff's Office parking lot. She barreled through the doors and found her husband sitting behind one of the desks in the open bull pen and staring intently at a computer screen. Caleb looked up at her expectantly.

"We need to get to Harley as fast as we can. There's a lady there who may have seen Emma."

**********

The key word in the message was "honey." While en route Jenny explained to Caleb that when Emma was very small, she couldn't pronounce "Jenny" or "Jennifer." When Emma had heard their mother refer to Jenny as "honey" - as all mothers sometimes do-, Emma, too, began calling her "Honey." The name stuck until Jenny hit her teens, when Jenny finally demanded that Emma quit embarrassing her in front of her friends by using that nickname.

Jenny determined the conversation between Emma and Mrs. Turney's grandson must have been Emma's way of getting a message to Jenny – a message her captor would never have understood.

Jenny suggested Caleb change into "civies" for the trip and that they drive her pickup, rather than an official

Pottawatomie Sheriff's vehicle. Jenny didn't want either Mrs. Turney or her grandson to know the real reason for their visit. People in the far southeastern part of the state were very reticent about any law enforcement official or, in truth, any outsider. Jenny was afraid that if Mrs. Turney knew Caleb was an undersheriff, and that they were searching for a kidnaper and his victim, she would shut up like a clam.

Caleb proposed he be the one to strike up a casual conversation with Mrs. Turney and her grandson to try to get as much information as he could. Caleb was a master at getting people to talk. Jenny would examine the dog. She was too uptight to pull off any casual conversation anyway.

**********

The vehicle had barely slid to a stop on the gravel at "Turney's Country Store" when Jenny jumped out and raced inside. In response to the bell above the front door, an elderly woman raised up slowly from behind the counter in the middle of the room. "Help you?" she asked.

"Are you Mrs. Turney? I'm Dr. Tallchief. We spoke this morning about your dog?"

"Right, right. Thank you so much for coming," she said emotionally. "Come on back." She waived them forward.

Jenny carefully threaded her way down the densely packed aisle. The store obviously stocked something for everyone – or maybe everything for anyone. There were food items, sporting goods, camping gear, some clothing and electronic movies and games. A large produce, meat and drink cooler extended down the entire left side of the room. In the center of the store was a counter holding an ancient cash register.

As Jenny walked towards Mrs. Turney, she held her medical bag close to her chest. She was afraid she would sideswipe something and send an entire aisle of dry goods or cans crashing down.

On the floor, a large mixed-breed chocolate Lab sprawled lackadaisically across a carefully made bed of blankets. The elderly proprietor moved to sit on a nearby stool giving Jenny room to examine the dog. Jenny immediately took in the lab's unhealthy appearance.

"Let's check you out, boy," Jenny intoned. Instantly, the lab's tail started to thump the floor and his head slightly lifted to look at Jenny. Later, Mrs. Turney would swear that Zeppy actually smiled.

As Jenny knelt down beside the animal, she pulled a stethoscope, a penlight, otoscope and thermometer from her medical bag and let the dog sniff each instrument in turn.

She noted the animal was underweight and his gums were tacky – sure sign of dehydration. Additionally, he had a poor hair coat, and he appeared to be weak and lethargic. As she gently stroked his fur, she sensed the lab's nausea, his thirst, and overriding exhaustion.

While Jenny continued her examination, Caleb bought a cold coke, leaned up against the counter and began a low key chat – about the weather, hunting and fishing in the woods around this part of Oklahoma, – just everything and anything to put the elderly woman at ease.

When the conversation turned to football, Craig Turney, her teenage grandson, shyly appeared in the doorway in the wall at the back of the store. Caleb encouraged him to join in the conversation and Craig reluctantly did so. After shaking hands, Caleb complimented the teenager on his red O.U. ball cap and the two discussed the Sooners chances for a national championship this year.

Mrs. Turney was at first closed-mouthed, but seeing that Jenny and her beloved Zeppy were getting along just fine, that Dr. Tallchief really did seem concerned about the animal's well-being, she relaxed. She was also impressed that Caleb was kind to Craig, too. Soon, like a waterfall, the words started to pour from the elderly woman's lips. The three talked about living in the country, raising her grandson, the store, and, finally, the kinds of strange customers who stopped by.

Jenny, although intently listening to the conversation, continued to carefully examine Zeppy. With some difficulty, the dog flipped over on his back for a thorough tummy-rub.

As Jenny gently caressed the soft belly fur, the distinctively sweet tobacco odor of marijuana came to her almost as though her fingers were holding it. She pulled her fingertips up to her nose, but the smell had vanished. When she again patted Zeppy's stomach, the evasive aroma returned. Puzzled, Jenny looked into Zeppy's large expressive brown eyes, and knew this smell had to mean something. But what?

In the meantime, Caleb had totally captivated both Mrs. Turney and her grandson. Mrs. Turney's arms moved in wide circles as she talked about the varied customer base of the Turney's Country Store and of the many trials and tribulations she endured as a store-owner.

To emphasize her point, Mrs. Turney mentioned a man who had recently come to the store. "As a matter of fact," she noted, "that was how I come to call the doctor about Zeppy."

"Oh?"

"A week ago today, Friday – yes – it was last Friday - about time to close up, this young man come in. He was all business – no time for chatter. He was stockin' up on all kinds of campin' gear, food, rifle shells, and toilet paper – just a lot of supplies. I figured he was goin' camping for a long time out here somewheres in the woods."

"Why did you think so?" asked Caleb.

"Well, the man," she thought a moment. "I do believe he did say something about a cabin. Yeah, now

I remember. He wanted to get there before sunset 'cause the cabin was hard to find at night, and it was pretty close to dark already."

Caleb nodded, but didn't interrupt.

Craig continued, "There was a lady with him waiting in the pickup outside. They was having some trouble with that old gas pump and I tried to help her. She was real pretty and nice. She sees Zeppy and she tells me about you, uh, I mean you," glancing at Jenny, "and asked me to say it back to her – so I wouldn't forget. She told me to call you right away."

Jenny stood up and asked Mrs. Turney whether Zeppy had had trouble with throwing up or diarrhea.

"Yeah, he does – but not all the time. And sometimes he won't eat at all. He seems to get better and then worse, she said and added, "He's been real worse lately."

Jenny asked Mrs. Turney if she could bring the lab to the Tecumseh Clinic as soon as possible, for some tests.

"You know, when Zeppy first got sick, we took him to the vet in Idabel. They done all kinds of tests – tests that cost a ton of money. They even checked for worms – *worms*, mind you. As if I'd let my Zeppy get worms. We take real good care of him – he's part of our family. He gets all his shots and heartworm pills every month. The Idabel vet give him a shot of something or other – and he did get better for a little while." She looked sadly at her ailing pet. "But now, he's worse again – much worse."

Mrs. Turney sighed, "What you're suggesting – all those tests – that sounds like it costs a lot of money. We already spent a whole lot of money and we ain't got much, you know?"

"Mrs. Turney, don't you worry about money. The honey cure is free. We'll take real good care of Zeppy, and if everything goes well, he should be better in no time." Jenny gently patted Mrs. Turney's shoulder to reassure her.

Jenny asked, "May I use your phone?"

"Surely you can, it's right here." Mrs. Turney's voice cracked a little and she pulled out a handkerchief to blow her nose.

Jenny picked up the land-line on the table behind the store's counter. Her cell phone was useless in this area of tall hills and deep valleys.

She dialed the Tecumseh Clinic and spoke to Annie in her most professional voice, "Annie, Mrs. Turney will be bringing in her dog, Zeppy, probably as soon as tomorrow. Will you please tell Dr. Martin to give him any tests and treatment the dog might need. Also, please ask Dr. Martin to look at the possibility that Zeppy has Addison's. I will take care of all charges under my honey cure project funds and there is to be no cost to Mrs. Turney for anything. I will call later to confirm all the details. This is a very special dog and he needs the very best of care."

Jenny replaced the receiver, leaving Annie sputtering with unanswered questions.

Tears rushed into the eyes and down the cheeks of the elderly, worn woman behind the counter. She clasped Jenny's hand between hers and said, "Bless you, miss. God bless you."

Jenny reached in her pocket for a business card to give Mrs. Turney. The elderly woman said she'd close the store and take Zeppy in the very next day – even if it was Saturday – her busiest day of the week.

Caleb and Jenny turned to leave and as if it were an afterthought, Jenny said, "Craig, I was listening to the story about the man and the woman at the store last week. What happened after the woman told you to call me?"

"Well, the man come rushing out of the store and yelled at me to get away from his pickup. He was real mad, but I hadn't done nothing but try to help! He grabbed me by my jacket and screamed in my face, asking what the lady had said. I told him the truth – nothin' but to call a vet."

"The lady - she told him to leave me alone. Then he got really mad at her and he said, 'I told you to keep quiet,' but she just said there was no need for a dog to suffer like that. The man backed off, sayin' something about how his momma was a dog-lover, too." Craig continued, "Then he whispered something in her face and they drove off fast."

"What did he say?"

"Don't know ….couldn't hear. But his face was all red and he was grittin' his teeth."

"Do you remember what the pickup looked like?"

Craig thought a minute. "It was an old white Chevy and – a mess. Old white '96 Chevy Silverado, rusted up and with a broke taillight. I was going to tell him about the taillight – but he give me a 'fuck you' look," Craig slid his eyes toward his grandmother. "Sorry, Granna. So I just come back in the store and told Granna what she said. We tried a bunch of times to call you, but that grouchy old woman in your office said you weren't there."

Caleb asked what the lady in the pickup looked like and Craig replied, "Her hair was all blonde - long and curly, and well, she had a real nice way of talking." Craig blushed.

"Oh - she waved 'bye' to me and I noticed she had a real big ring on this finger," he held up his right hand index finger, "– a big "E" with diamonds all over it."

Mrs. Turney concluded with a large sigh, "Even though it was the best sale I had all week, I hope he never comes back. That man give me the willies." Craig nodded in agreement.

\*\*\*\*\*\*\*\*\*\*

Although the two were eager to formulate a search plan based on their new information, they bade the two Turneys a warm goodbye, crossed the store's interior and out onto the wide porch separating the Turney's Country Store from its graveled parking area in front.

As Jenny climbed into the SUV and began to pull the passenger door closed, Mrs. Turney poked her head out of the screen door and gestured for them to rejoin her on the porch.

As they came close, she looked around conspiratorially, lowered her voice, and said, "You know, I ain't as much an old fool as some might think." She cast a shrewd eye in Caleb's and then Jenny's direction, "but I know you're looking for that man and that woman from last Friday. I know somethin's goin' on, and I don't want to know what. I got my own troubles. I usual don't put my nose where it don't belong, but you both – you're good people. That little lady Craig was talking to - she's good people, too, and I'm guessing she's in trouble."

Caleb and Jenny exchanged glances and nodded.

Mrs. Turney took a large breath and her voice got even lower, "Well, – that man – he looked real familiar to me and it finally come to me why....I believe he's old Sherman Tyler's boy. Them Tylers are real bad business. They own a lot of land hereabouts and grow marijuana all over it."

"Believe me," her voice got even lower, "They'd just as soon kill you as look at you. Many's the one who's disappeared after crossing one of 'em.

"Can't rightly remember the name of the son for the life of me, but Sherm Tyler, he had a cabin somewhere off East End Road, about four miles east off Highway

3. I think the cabin might be back in the woods quite a bit, but I'm not really sure. That may be where they was headed. You didn't hear none of this from me ---but, *please, please,* be real careful."

# Chapter 22

"Caleb, it's her. It has to be her. Nobody else has that gaudy rhinestone ring with the "E" initial. And, Zeppy - he was trying to tell me about the marijuana connection. We have to call the local sheriff and the OSBI right now. Surely, they'll know exactly where the cabin is and can send in some deputies. He's had her now for more than a week.....we just have to get her back." Jenny's voice was rapid and frantic.

"Jen, the sheriff still doesn't have any tangible evidence that the Tylers were involved in Emma's kidnapping. Plus, the OSBI is in charge – he wouldn't have any authority to do anything without their okay. Bottom line – he can't send in any of his men – especially into a potentially dangerous situation – without something more. Let me call him and see what we can find out."

Caleb veered over on the shoulder and tried his cell phone. Luck was with him and he got through to the

Sheriff himself, Jim Grace. Caleb filled the Sheriff in on Emma's disappearance and the conversation he and Jenny had had with Mrs. Turney. Luckily, Sheriff Grace was already aware of the situation, having read Caleb's inquiries on the association's list serve.

A former Oklahoma City police detective, Sheriff Grace was as sharp as he was politically astute. He recognized the danger for Emma, but he also knew there wasn't much he could do at this point. No way could he get a warrant – especially against the Tylers who were so solidly connected. Although he would dearly love to put one or more of those sons-of-bitches behind bars – or in the ground - there wasn't a whole lot he could do at this point except share background information.

Caleb learned the Tylers were notorious in this part of the state. There was the old man, Sherman, and three sons, Jacob, Chad and John. Mary, the mother, had passed away many years before as a result of a one-car accident. The previous sheriff thought the circumstances of her death to be somewhat suspicious; however, the county coroner deemed it purely accidental. At the time no one seemed to be concerned that the coroner was a distant relative of the Tylers. Since the sheriff was left with no real evidence, and then surprisingly declined to run for reelection, the whole matter was put to rest.

Jacob and Chad, both married, had been arrested several times for a variety of offenses, including drugs, domestic abuse and murder, but neither had ever been convicted or even gone to trial. Somehow, witnesses either changed their stories or just conveniently disappeared.

John, on the other hand, was an unknown. He'd never been in trouble – at least as far as the sheriff knew. He was almost reclusive - never seen in town or any of the local hang-outs.

The Tylers owned a large swath of land covering approximately 1500 acres in McCurtain County. The Sheriff himself had never set foot on most of it. They also owned two '96 Chevy Silverados. But then so did half of the residents of McCurtain County.

The Tyler family lived in a secluded enclave of four homes located just outside Harley proper and set on a high hill overlooking the valley. None could be the house Caleb was looking for; however, the Sheriff did know that the family maintained several small cabins in various corners of their land holdings. One of these cabins might be the one Mrs. Turney was speaking of.

Sheriff Grace agreed to drive over to the main house and see if he could get an exact location for any of the cabins. But he warned, "Don't hold your breath, Caleb. These people are as mean and as secretive as they come."

# Chapter 23

John entered the woods to the northwest of the cabin's front door, and followed a well-traveled path toward his "special place." It was in that special place John kept the remains of his former fiancés. He would occasionally visit them to relive their time together or even discuss the pros and cons of a new potential wife. John usually enjoyed visiting – even more so when he was planning to add another to their group.

But this time was different, he thought. He'd really thought Jenna was the one. It was so wrong to betray someone who loved you so much. Unforgivably wrong.

As he dug her grave, he considered how he would hunt Jenna. The others had been easy. He smiled as he recalled his first – or was it the second – woman he had brought here. When she failed him and he turned her loose for the hunt, she actually ran straight down the road. She was so stupid, he killed her right away. Nobody should be that stupid.

Jenna would not be stupid – but she also wouldn't know the woods. He was certain she'd give him a fine chase. When he finally brought her down, he wouldn't kill her straight away. He'd play with her for a while – maybe even taste what she had between her legs. He'd teach her not to fool with his love. Oh, Jenna. Why did you have to be just like the rest?

The more John thought about the hunt and the subsequent fun he would have with his now-dishonored ex-fiancé, the more excited he became. He wanted to start the hunt right away, but that wouldn't be right. One had to begin the hunt in the early morning hours – just as the sun was coming up. That was the fitting way to play – and he wanted Jenna's death to be just right.

# Chapter 24

Early morning mists enveloped the SUV in a blanket of quiet and foreboding. A hint of the coming sunrise infused the light filtering through the windshield and into Jenny's partially open eyes.

Jesse stirred in the seat behind her, opened one eye as if to say, "You've got to be kidding me," snorted, and rolled over. Caleb snored softly in the fully-reclined front passenger seat.

The previous night had not gone well. Sheriff Grace had spoken with Sherman Tyler, but learned nothing useful. The Sheriff told Caleb he would go to the McCurtain County Courthouse the next morning to see if he could find any land deeds with cabins listed as part of the property, but it would be a long, time-consuming search and he may well come up with nothing.

Jenny insisted she and Caleb continue to look on their own. Caleb attempted to convince Jenny to wait – to develop some kind of search strategy with his brothers and the Sheriff, but Jenny would have none of it. She was adamant that she and Caleb at least drive the length of East End Road to scc if they could find anything.

From the top of the highest hill they could find, Caleb was able to get a weak signal on his cell phone. He called his brother, Matt, and told him to bring all the Tallchief brothers to the intersection of East End Road and Highway 3 by 6:00 the next morning to help in the search. He did not need to tell them to come armed.

Jenny called Doc and briefed him about Zeppy. She told him she suspected hypoadrenocorticism and recommended blood work, including an electrolyte panel, ACTH stim test, fluids and a steroid injection. She told Doc she'd pay for everything herself. Doc assured her he'd contact Mrs. Turney personally and arrange for her to bring Zeppy in to the Clinic. He'd make sure the animal had everything he needed. If Jenny's diagnosis was correct, he'd also set the dog up for routine medications and follow-up. He further told Jenny not to be silly about the money, the Clinic would cover the cost of everything. He signed off by telling her not to worry about anything at the Clinic – just be careful and find Emma.

Caleb tried to raise the McCurtain County Sheriff again to let him know of the plan to explore East End Road, but the signal had mysteriously vanished.

Jenny, Caleb, and Jesse eventually found an old signpost that appeared to say "East End Rd" in old and battered lettering. They followed it and explored several small dirt roads crossing East End, if one could call them roads, until darkness and fatigue halted their search. They found no new tracks, no further hints or clues to Emma's whereabouts.

Twinges of desperation clouded Jenny's mind just before she nodded off. "All in all," she thought, "another day lost."

**********

Jenny woke with the same thought on her mind. "Lost day or not, nature calls," Jenny whispered to herself.

She quietly opened the truck door, and slipped out onto the cool, damp earth, pulling her jacket behind her. She patted the pocket to make sure the small flashlight she always carried was there. "That's all I need – to fall and break a leg," thought Jenny morosely as she stepped into the predawn mist. Jenny opened the door for Jesse, who'd apparently decided it was not too early for a bathroom visit, after all.

The "road" here was only an earthen lane – two somewhat parallel ribbons of moldy, rock-strewn mud, totally hemmed in on each side by the encroaching woodlands. It was impossible to know what lay just five feet into those unforgiving walls of timber, rock and brush. It could be a small stream or a herd of wild animals or a hidden field of marijuana. No way to tell. The only thing easy to tell was that this was a very lonely and dangerous part of the state. That thought only made her more despondent.

Spying a nearby potential bathroom by the faint gleam of her flashlight, Jenny carefully picked her way through the underbrush and slid behind a tree. As she came to her feet while rearranging her clothing, she felt, rather than saw, a presence in the grey morning light. Standing just a few yards away, a yearling stared directly at her – neither coming closer nor fleeing at Jenny's movements. The animal did not flinch at Jesse's presence but continued its unblinking gaze. A thin thread of electricity tingled down Jenny's spine and, as her eyes met those of the deer, those deep pools of brown intellect told her that she should follow.

The three picked their way through the ever-thickening brush – the yearling in the lead with Jenny and Jesse close behind. Low hanging branches slapped Jenny in the face and upper body and her feet were constantly attacked by the vines and stickers covering the forest floor.

After what seemed an eternity, the deer came to a sudden, full stop and Jenny quietly moved up beside her. Spread out in front of the three was a somewhat circular clearing, and centered in the clearing was a sturdy stone and wood-sided cabin, a shed, and rusty white Chevy pickup with a broken right taillight.

Jenny held her breath. The only sign of life was a

very faint glow seen through the single opaque window on the front of the cabin. Everything was silent.

Jenny froze. Time stopped.

Finally, with a step, the yearling broke the spell. She moved forward into the opening and began to graze slowly around the perimeter of the clearing, occasionally raising her head, acutely in tune with the natural rhythm and flow of her world.

Jenny, too, quickly assessed her current situation. Although she knew she should go back for Caleb, she couldn't bring herself to leave, if, in fact, Emma was in that cabin. She had to know, she had to be sure.

She slowly worked her way around the edge of the clearing until she was close enough to duck-walk up to the window. She slowly eased herself up until she could see inside.

The faint light in the room came from some night lighting in the kitchen and the glow of embers in the fireplace. As she watched, Jenny was able to see a man rise from a large chair in front of the fireplace and approach the bed. Jenny was at first terrified the man had seen her outside the window. But he apparently had other reasons for moving. He disappeared into a door at the far side of the room. A shadow moved on the bed.

Suddenly the bathroom door opened, backlighting a medium-sized, well-built man. He strode over to the bed and jerked the woman into full view. It was Emma.

"Oh my God, it's Emma," Jenny almost shouted out loud. Emma appeared to be awake and fully dressed.

The man threw a coat at her and she slowly retrieved it from the floor and put her arms into the sleeves. The man was talking in a low voice, but Jenny could not make out his words.

Jenny bent over low and whispered into Jesse's ear, "Jesse, get Caleb! Hurry, girl, hurry!"

Jesse looked solemnly at Jenny and then quietly turned and disappeared into the predawn light. When Jesse was out of sight, Jenny silently stole around the side of the cabin to await her chance to get her sister out of there.

After an interminable few minutes, Jenny heard voices and movement within the cabin, and finally a muted squeak of the door opening. Tyler stepped out on the small porch and looked carefully over the landscape. In his right hand, he held a rifle.

Within view of the front porch and just in front of the shed's door, the yearling continued to pick her way through the foliage. She had, since Jenny's arrival at the cabin, been joined by two other deer. All three stopped eating and turned in unison at the sound of the door, but sensing no danger, one at a time dropped their heads to the ground.

Jenny heard a deep, angry voice mutter, "Okay, okay, let's go – I'll give you ten minutes head start. You don't deserve it, but I'm a fair man."

More rattling, and finally footsteps. Jenny had no idea what she was going to do, but she sure as hell wasn't going to leave without her sister.

As the disembodied footsteps approached the side of the cabin closest to the shed and the grazing animals, the decision of what to do next was suddenly taken from Jenny's hands.

The largest of the three deer bolted and ran headlong into the man, knocking him to the ground and sending his 30-30 skittering across the wet weeds and into the underbrush.

Needing no further incentive, Jenny launched from her hiding place and grabbed her sister by the hand. It took no more than a microsecond for Emma to recognize the woman yanking her forward was her beloved Jenny. Holding onto one another, they flew across the clearing and back into the woods, heading for Caleb, Jesse, and safety.

Completely baffled by the chain of events, Tyler remained stunned on the ground - shaking his head and trying to make sense of what had just happened. As he rose to his knees, he saw, with a mixture of shock and disbelief, Jenny and Emma disappearing into the obscurity of the fog-enveloped woods.

Tyler raised his hands to the heavens and screamed in frustration, "You bitch, you bitch - you're just like the others… a man can't trust any woman…"

Rage quickly replaced confusion as he spun around on his knees in circles in a frantic search for his rifle. Not even taking the time to stand up, Tyler shuffled across the clearing on his hands and knees until he had his hands wrapped around the gun butt. He stood, flicked off the safety, cocked the gun and aimed it in the general direction of the fleeing figures. He fired.

The boom of the rifle shattered the tranquility of the morning, but the shot did not even come close to its targets. Tyler did not intend it to. He wanted those crazy, defiant bitches to be scared shitless and to know he was coming for them.

As a flurry of four-letter descriptors erupted from his mouth, Tyler brushed himself off and ran into the shack for more rifle shells and, most importantly, for his special hunting knife. He would need that. He would make both of them pay for their wickedness – their lying ways. All women were wicked creatures. They said they loved you – and then they ran off. It had happened to him just too many times in the past. Well, it wouldn't go unpunished. It hadn't before and it wouldn't now.

And, this time, there were two to pay the price.

Fully armed, Tyler resolutely set off after the sisters. Hatred blazed in his eyes and vengeance burned in his belly.

\*\*\*\*\*\*\*\*\*\*

The reverberation from the rifle blast echoed through the forest and brought Caleb instantly awake. "Oh, shit" Caleb voiced the panic he felt. "Where's Jenny? Where's Jesse?"

Caleb retrieved his sidearm from the locked glove

box then tumbled from the pickup and ran to the back to get his rifle out of the locking tool box. He was still standing at the back of the pickup when Jesse burst from the underbrush.

She barked furiously at Caleb to follow and in the same fluid movement executed a 180 – degree turn, leaping back into the dense underbrush. The German shepherd was already far ahead when Caleb entered the thicket in her wake, running and stumbling helter-skelter towards the ominous sound.

# Chapter 25

Jenny and Emma ran blindly through the snarling underbrush and low hanging branches. Jenny held up one arm to fend off the woodlands and held tightly with the other to her sister. No way was she going to let Emma go. Small twigs and large branches slapped relentlessly against her face and arms. Sticker bush seeds hitched a ride on every exposed expanse of clothing or skin.

"Run, run," Jenny cried frantically, as they tripped and fell their way into the claustrophobic black before them. Losing all sense of direction, they pushed forward, running – running - until the adrenalin of their escape began to wane.

Emma begged Jenny to stop – just for a moment – to let her catch her breath. "Surely he can't find us now," Emma wheezed.

Both women dropped to the ground, hugging, crying, laughing and holding tight to one another. The words tumbled out. Each talked over the other – neither listening to the words – but celebrating in the love and relief they felt.

"I thought I was going to die," Emma cried.

"Emma, we've been frantic. Everyone has been trying to find you…"

"But you did," reasoned Emma. "I thought I was going to die, but you found me. I should have known you'd find me."

"We're not out of the woods yet," Jenny said, smiling at her own bad joke.

Emma groaned.

"Come on, we can't stop until we find Caleb and get away from here."

Jenny pulled Emma to her feet and hand-in-hand dashed through a small opening in the trees. She stopped up short when the two emerged onto a rugged embankment about five feet high. Below a rock-strewn stream raged with snow melt-off and ice.

"Oh God," said Jenny, frantically looking all around. "I don't remember crossing this stream on the way to the cabin. Maybe we're turned around."

Jenny looked frenetically for a familiar group of trees or … something – anything - to tell them which way to run.

Across the stream, blackness beckoned. Emma thought she could make out a rise in the landscape, maybe a mound or the foot of a hill, but she couldn't be sure.

Suddenly and quite close to them, Jenny and Emma

heard the shout of their pursuer. Obviously, John Tyler was not trying to mask his approach. He wanted them to know he was coming.

As fast as they could, they stumbled down the embankment and ran across the frigid water. They clawed their way up the far side of the streambed, and entered the darkness of the woods beyond. They climbed up the rise in the hillside and hunkered down in the center of a dense growth of shoulder-high brush.

Almost as soon as the sisters had disappeared from view, a male voice clearly called out,

"Oh bitches, come out – come out now. You've been very bad and I'm coming for you."

How could Tyler have found them so fast?

**********

Caleb had followed Jesse as closely as he could, but the shepherd galloped so far ahead he often lost sight of her. When he finally emerged into a clearing, he saw a small cabin and the white '96 pickup they had been searching for.

His heart sunk to his heels. Jenny had been right – Emma and her captor had been close by. Caleb was terrified the killer now had both sisters in his grasp and he prayed he would not be too late.

Still on Jenny's trail, Jesse leaped into the woods on the north side of the clearing. She began to emit an eerie howl – one Caleb had never heard before – and one that chilled his spine. The howl intensified as the dog raced through the brush.

Caleb sprinted to close the gap.

**********

John Tyler emerged on the bank of the small stream just as Jenny and Emma melted into the darkness of the dense woods on its far side.

He could not see them – nor did he know how close they were. But he did know they had come this way. He could see their tracks in the mud and where they had climbed up the embankment on the other side. Just in case they were within hearing range, he thought he'd shake them up a bit.

"I know you're there – both of you," he yelled. "This is kind of a treat for me, you know. Two for the price of one."

Tyler chuckled as he prepared to launch forward across the stream bed, sure it would only be a few minutes before he had his prey in sight.

Just as he leaned forward into his stride, he heard crashing of the underbrush and an odd howling noise just behind and to his right. As he turned to ascertain the cause of the sound, Jesse burst over the embankment and knocked Tyler down into the water.

"Goddam it, what is it with you animals?" John struggled to regain his footing and his rifle.

At full speed, Jesse dashed on past him through the stream, up the far side of the bank and disappeared into the woods beyond. It only took her a few minutes to find Jenny and Emma, who were still hiding in the thicket.

"Oh, Jesse, thank God" Jenny whispered, standing and hugging the animal to her. "Take us to Caleb. Get us out of here. Hurry, hurry!"

John, finally vertical, began screaming obscenities and turning in circles. He yelled until he was out of breath. At last, he seemed to regain a little of his former composure and began to slowly follow in the dog's trail – rifle in one hand and hunting knife in the other.

\*\*\*\*\*\*\*\*\*\*

Instead of leading the women away, Jesse hunkered further down into the thicket. The dog grabbed Jenny's jacket front and forced her into a squat.

"Jesse," Jenny whispered urgently, "What are you doing? We've got to go!" From their wooded shelter, the two women could clearly see their pursuer standing mid-stream below.

Emma turned to run, but Jenny held tight to her sister's coat.

"Jen, he's coming!" Emma whispered urgently. "You don't know how crazy this bastard is! He's killed other women and he'll kill us both. He'll kill Jesse, too. We've got to get out of here – now!"

"Emma, trust Jesse. She's telling us to stay hidden. To stay down. She knows something we don't."

Emma, terror reflected in her eyes, paused and then slowly lowered herself to the ground. She willed her breathing to slow and, like Jenny, suddenly noticed a marked change in their surroundings. Somehow Emma could hear more acutely, and what she heard was the absolute silence. No animals – no birds. Even the burble from the stream below seemed muted. It was as if a magician had cast a spell to slow time and sound.

After a moment, Emma thought she could make out one distinctive sound - someone moving through the underbrush from the direction Jesse had come. And the sound was getting louder and louder.

John Tyler, too, heard the noise. He turned mid-stream, brought up his rifle, and fired in one easy motion, just as Caleb topped the embankment. The shot ripped through the early morning air, and Caleb fell. He pitched forward, sliding down the dirt mound toward the water. Jenny's husband lay face-down and still by the water's edge.

"Oh, my God. Caleb!" Jenny whimpered as she tried to jump up. Caleb did not stir – Jenny could not see if he was breathing.

"Oh my God. Oh, my God."

Jesse would not allow Jenny to move. When she tried, the shepherd would just clamp more tightly on

Jenny's coat. "Wait, wait" she seemed to be urgently conveying.

For some reason, Jenny thought of Paul White Horse. She reached into her coat pocket and grasped the talisman he had given her. She forced herself to center her thoughts – to breathe deeply and slowly and remember the old man's words.

"Trust," he had said. Jenny took a deep breath. "Okay, okay," Jenny thought. She looped her arm around Jesse's neck. She would trust.

As Jenny held tight to Jesse and Emma, the thicket to her left stirred just slightly – almost like an exhaled breath. Moving stealthily but surely, a huge grey coyote floated past them – curiously glancing in their direction and then turning back toward the stream. Even in the dim light, Jenny would tell this creature was much larger and huskier than any coyote she had ever seen before. Emma, too, saw the animal. Her hand pressed to her mouth and her eyes grew wide with fear and amazement.

At the foot of the embankment, John approached Caleb's still body.

"Well, what have we here? He kicked Caleb over on his back. "Our knight in shining armor?"

Tyler glanced up and down the stream for any signs of the women – still not sure just where his intended victims were hiding.

He shouted, "Sorry, ladies. Looks like the fair

maidens are not going to be rescued this time." Tyler looked at Caleb again.

"How about if we finish this up, Sir Knight?" Tyler laughed, loud and shrill, and brought his rifle up for the kill shot.

In that instant, almost as if he had been hit by an electric shock, John Tyler sensed danger. He quickly turned and frantically scanned each side of the stream. Although the small patch of sky over the water had lightened slightly, John still was unable to discern what lie just beyond the tree line on either side. The woods were a study in shades of black and gray.

At first, nothing. As Tyler carefully searched the perimeter, he could neither hear nor see any threat. Then from his left came a single low grumble, joined by a second and then a third. Then began the howls. In an instant, a multitude of growls and howls joined together until the entire streambed vibrated with sound at a deafening level.

As Emma and Jenny watched from their hidden sanctuary, John took several stumbling steps toward them. But he was not searching for them – he was trying to determine the location of the threat.

Here and there Jenny thought she could make out sets of luminous eyes just beyond view in the woods on the far side of the stream. Pair after pair appeared. John Tyler was turning in a continuous circle now, terrified, but unsure whether he should move forward or backward. He could not ascertain the direction from which the threat emanated. It seemed to be everywhere at once. Menace oozed from every tree – every bush.

Jenny and Emma, too, recognized a heightened sense of foreboding in the woods – but for some reason they were not afraid. It almost seemed the air around them had become thick with anger. The wind had fallen away. Even the trees seemed to hold their collective breath.

Then, as if in an explosion, large feral creatures leapt from the woods on both sides of the stream – two great surges of grey crashing forward like opposing tidal waves.

John Tyler twisted from the impact of the first coyote and fired off a wild shot. Then all the women could see was the frantic slashing of John's knife in a whirl of grey as the madman tried to carve out a path of escape. All they could hear was the furious growling and yapping of the hoard and broken semi-human screams.

After what seemed an interminable amount of time, the sounds trailed off, then stilled. John Tyler could no longer be seen. Coyotes stood immobile for a moment almost as if paying homage to their fallen comrades. Then they silently drifted back into the darkness from which they had come.

The horrible magic of the moment broke like a glass shattering on a cold, marble floor. Jenny ran to Caleb. He was breathing, but the bullet had caught his shoulder, and he'd lost a lot of blood. Amazingly, none of the wild animals appeared to have touched her wounded husband. Jenny stripped off her shirt and bound his shoulder as best she could.

Emma and Jesse slowly walked over to what remained of John Tyler. He was no longer recognizable as a human being. He had been torn limb from limb, his face obliterated and his throat shredded. His rifle was no where to be seen, but the fingers of his one remaining hand were still clutched around his hunting knife.

Strewn about the site were two coyote bodies, one still quivering in its death throes. A third held watch over its dying companion.

# Chapter 26

Caleb didn't remember much after he followed Jesse through the cabin's clearing and into the woods. He spent a week in the hospital in Idabel with Jenny at his side. Toward the end of the week Sheriff Holcomb was visiting when Special Agent Eric McBride sauntered in. "Thought you might like to know what's going on down by Harley."

The OSBI had been very busy. They'd investigated both the cabin and the surrounding wooded area. Nine bodies were located by cadaver dogs – likely previous fiancés. Four of the victims were from Oklahoma, Marcy Ford and Stephanie Rushing were among those whose bodies had been identified. There were two women from Texas and the remaining three were still unidentified. Apparently, John had been "shopping" for the perfect wife for a very long time.

There was also one empty grave – one which had

recently been dug. McBride did not have to explain just how close they had come to losing Emma forever.

With a warrant for John's home in the family compound, the OSBI agents had found enough evidence and, in conjunction with the Oklahoma Bureau of Narcotics, raided seven marijuana fields on Tyler land. And, since the property was owned by Sherman and his sons together with John, they were able to bring charges against the entire family.

Sheriff Grace was a very happy man. This time, he felt sure, the charges would stick. John's network was dismantled with several drug arrests made throughout southeastern and central Oklahoma. Several 'illegals' were among those arrested and would be sent to ICE as soon as the OSBI and the OBN were through with them.

Emma had been able to fill in some of the gaps from things John had said to her during her captivity and the bits and pieces she had found in the cabin. For example, John told Emma he wanted his future wife to be as pretty as his mother had been – thus he had looked for women who were like her physically. And since his mother had gone to college, his perfect wife would also have to be a college student.

According to the OSBI, John used several methods to "find" candidates for his perfect wife. One method was the grief seminars; another was to hack into the counseling files of local colleges. He looked for girls who had no close family members. That way, no one would miss them or keep looking for them. Apparently these methods had worked just fine. Just fine, that is, until he chose Emma.

As Eric McBride pulled on his coat to leave, he handed Caleb a sealed padded envelope. "Open this after I'm gone, okay?"

Then he said his goodbyes to Jenny and Sheriff Holcomb, tipping his fingertips to his forehead in a mock salute as he left.

With Jenny's help, Caleb ripped open the envelope. Holcomb moved closer to the bed so he, too, could see what the package contained. Inside was a photograph of David Sable and Charlie Bishop. Bishop had one arm across Sable's shoulder and the two appeared to be in deep conversation. The attached note read,

> Caleb,
>
> One of our undercover agents took this photo outside a Bishop-owned cattle auction building in far southwest Oklahoma.
>
> Confidentially, Charlie Bishop has been under OSBI surveillance for quite some time because of his suspected involvement in a number of illegal activities – including cattle rustling. The OSBI plans to arrest him in the next couple of days.
>
> Nobody could identify the second man in the photo – but I thought I remembered seeing him – or somebody who looked an awful lot like him in your office. I did some checking and found that

your new deputy sheriff, David Sable, was born out of wedlock to an intern who once worked for Charlie Bishop. Sable's mom married a couple of years later and David was adopted by the new husband. Interestingly however; David Sable, whose high school grades were nothing to shout about, received a full-ride college scholarship from the Bishop Foundation.

Coincidence???? Or maybe the Bishop-Sable connection is how the rustlers knew which ranches to hit – and which to avoid.

Eric

P.S. When you look closely, father and son look quite a bit alike, don't you think?

\*\*\*\*\*\*\*\*\*\*

Matt drove Caleb and Jenny home from the hospital. "How alike they are," thought Jenny, as Matt helped his big brother out of the jeep and into the house. Since the stairs were a little too much for Caleb to tackle at this point in his recovery, Jenny had turned the downstairs bedroom into Caleb's recovery room. That way, he'd be close to the downstairs bathroom, the kitchen and the big screen television. Not that Caleb would need to do anything for himself. His family had volunteered to stand watch day and night over the next few weeks to make sure Caleb didn't overdo. Caleb shoo'ed his family and all their good intentions away, however, because all he wanted was Jenny.

That evening, Jenny and Caleb sat talking in the quiet of their home. Clue, the grey and white kitten, and Curly Joe, the fugitive white puppy from Muskogee, wrestled and ran laps around the room. They'd named the kitten Clue because he'd led them to the grief seminar and Curly Joe – well, because no other name seemed to fit as perfectly. The two chased toys, each other, and occasionally jumped straight up apparently from the sheer joy of living. Paul White Horse would probably comment that adults could learn a lot from the young.

Jesse snoozed placidly at the foot of the bed, occasionally raising one eyelid to keep watch over the newest additions to her family. Her tired expression seemed to say, "Where in the world do they get their energy?"

Emma was out with Matt. Matt had determined Emma would not be out of his sight. Jenny wasn't sure how long Emma would tolerate Matt's hovering, but that was her problem. They'd work it out.

Jenny sat on the side of the bed and picked up Caleb's hand. "Caleb, I've never been so afraid in my life as when I saw Tyler's bullet hit you," she said, tears filling her eyes. "I knew in that moment that nothing was as important as the love we share. I was so afraid I'd never be able to tell you that."

She continued, her voice becoming almost a

whisper. "I know the last few months have been really hard on you, but I want you to know that I love you more than life itself." Jenny looked down at their intertwined fingers.

Caleb had no words which would in any way describe what he felt. He just leaned forward and wrapped his uninjured arm around his beloved wife and held her tight.

This time Jenny didn't even try to pull away.

# About the Author...

E.H. McEachern holds a doctorate in Higher Education Administration from Oklahoma State University. Serving as a teacher, administrator and as Assistant Vice-President for Curriculum and Policy in regional public universities, she retired from academic life after more than thirty years of serving students.

Being energetic and focused, Dr. McEachern has found retirement to be a springboard for various ventures and activities including; charity fund raising, traveling and miniature doll house construction. She is an avid reader of mystery, science fiction and novels of international intrigue.

The *Jenny Tallchief* series is the result of some two years of thoughtful research and planning.

Dr. McEachern and her husband live in Edmond, Oklahoma where she continues to spoil their Lhasa Apso, *Maggie*.